My Sweetheart

War Torn Letters Series, Volume 1

Lexy Timms

Published by Dark Shadow Publishing, 2019.

This is a work of fiction. Similarities to real people, places, or events are entirely coincidental.

MY SWEETHEART

First edition. July 31, 2019.

Copyright © 2019 Lexy Timms.

Written by Lexy Timms.

Also by Lexy Timms

A Burning Love Series
Spark of Passion
Flame of Desire
Blaze of Ecstasy

A Chance at Forever Series
Forever Perfect
Forever Desired
Forever Together

A "Kind of" Billionaire
Taking a Risk
Safety in Numbers
Pretend You're Mine

BBW Romance Series
Capturing Her Beauty
Pursuing Her Dreams

Tracing Her Curves

Beating the Biker Series
Making Her His
Making the Break
Making of Them

Billionaire Banker Series
Banking on Him
Price of Passion
Investing in Love
Knowing Your Worth
Treasured Forever
Banking on Christmas

Billionaire Holiday Romance Series
Driving Home for Christmas
The Valentine Getaway
Cruising Love

Billionaire in Disguise Series
Facade
Illusion
Charade

Billionaire Secrets Series
The Secret
Freedom
Courage
Trust
Impulse
Billionaire Secrets Box Set Books #1-3

Branded Series
Money or Nothing
What People Say
Give and Take

Building Billions
Building Billions - Part 1
Building Billions - Part 2
Building Billions - Part 3

Change of Heart Series
The Heart Needs
The Heart Wants
The Heart Knows

Conquering Warrior Series

Ruthless

Counting the Billions
Counting the Days
Counting On You
Counting the Kisses

Diamond in the Rough Anthology
Billionaire Rock
Billionaire Rock - part 2

Dominating PA Series
Her Personal Assistant - Part 1
Her Personal Assistant Box Set

Fake Billionaire Series
Faking It
Temporary CEO
Caught in the Act
Never Tell A Lie
Fake Christmas
Fake Billionaire Box Set #1-3

Firehouse Romance Series

Caught in Flames
Burning With Desire
Craving the Heat
Firehouse Romance Complete Collection

For His Pleasure
Elizabeth
Georgia
Madison

Fortune Riders MC Series
Billionaire Biker
Billionaire Ransom
Billionaire Misery

Fragile Series
Fragile Touch
Fragile Kiss
Fragile Love

Hades' Spawn Motorcycle Club
One You Can't Forget
One That Got Away
One That Came Back
One You Never Leave
One Christmas Night

Hades' Spawn MC Complete Series

Hard Rocked Series
Rhyme
Harmony
Lyrics

Heart of Stone Series
The Protector
The Guardian
The Warrior

Heart of the Battle Series
Celtic Viking
Celtic Rune
Celtic Mann
Heart of the Battle Series Box Set

Heistdom Series
Master Thief
Goldmine
Diamond Heist
Smile For Me

Highlander Wolf Series
Pack Run
Pack Land
Pack Rules

Just About Series
About Love
About Truth
About Forever

Justice Series
Seeking Justice
Finding Justice
Chasing Justice
Pursuing Justice
Justice - Complete Series

Kissed by Billions
Kissed by Passion
Kissed by Desire
Kissed by Love

Love You Series
Love Life

Need Love
My Love

Managing the Billionaire
Never Enough
Worth the Cost
Secret Admirers
Chasing Affection
Pressing Romance
Timeless Memories

Managing the Bosses Series
The Boss
The Boss Too
Who's the Boss Now
Love the Boss
I Do the Boss
Wife to the Boss
Employed by the Boss
Brother to the Boss
Senior Advisor to the Boss
Forever the Boss
Christmas With the Boss
Billionaire in Control
Billionaire Makes Millions
Billionaire at Work
Precious Little Thing
Priceless Love
Gift for the Boss - Novella 3.5
Managing the Bosses Box Set #1-3

Model Mayhem Series
Shameless
Modesty
Imperfection

Moment in Time
Highlander's Bride
Victorian Bride
Modern Day Bride
A Royal Bride
Forever the Bride

My Best Friend's Sister
Hometown Calling
A Perfect Moment
Thrown in Together

Neverending Dream Series
Neverending Dream - Part 1
Neverending Dream - Part 2
Neverending Dream - Part 3
Neverending Dream - Part 4
Neverending Dream - Part 5

Outside the Octagon
Submit
Fight
Knockout

Protecting Diana Series
Her Bodyguard
Her Defender
Her Champion
Her Protector
Her Forever

Protecting Layla Series
His Mission
His Objective
His Devotion

Racing Hearts Series
Rush
Pace
Fast

Reverse Harem Series
Primals

Archaic
Unitary

RIP Series
Track the Ripper
Hunt the Ripper
Pursue the Ripper

R&S Rich and Single Series
Alex Reid
Parker

Saving Forever
Saving Forever - Part 1
Saving Forever - Part 2
Saving Forever - Part 3
Saving Forever - Part 4
Saving Forever - Part 5
Saving Forever - Part 6
Saving Forever Part 7
Saving Forever - Part 8
Saving Forever Boxset Books #1-3

Shifting Desires Series
Jungle Heat
Jungle Fever

Jungle Blaze

Southern Romance Series
Little Love Affair
Siege of the Heart
Freedom Forever
Soldier's Fortune

Spanked Series
Passion
Playmate
Pleasure

Spelling Love Series
The Author
The Book Boyfriend
The Words of Love

Taboo Wedding Series
He Loves Me Not
With This Ring
Happily Ever After

Tattooist Series

Confession of a Tattooist
Surrender of a Tattooist
Heart of a Tattooist
Hopes & Dreams of a Tattooist

Tennessee Romance
Whisky Lullaby
Whisky Melody
Whisky Harmony

The Bad Boy Alpha Club
Battle Lines - Part 1
Battle Lines

The Brush Of Love Series
Every Night
Every Day
Every Time
Every Way
Every Touch

The Debt
The Debt: Part 1 - Damn Horse
The Debt: Complete Collection

The Fire Inside Series
Dare Me
Defy Me
Burn Me

The Golden Mail
Hot Off the Press
Extra! Extra!
Read All About It
Stop the Press
Breaking News
This Just In

The Lucky Billionaire Series
Lucky Break
Streak of Luck
Lucky in Love

The Sound of Breaking Hearts Series
Disruption
Destroy
Devoted

The University of Gatica Series

The Recruiting Trip
Faster
Higher
Stronger
Dominate
No Rush
University of Gatica - The Complete Series

T.N.T. Series
Troubled Nate Thomas - Part 1
Troubled Nate Thomas - Part 2
Troubled Nate Thomas - Part 3

Undercover Series
Perfect For Me
Perfect For You
Perfect For Us

Unknown Identity Series
Unknown
Unpublished
Unexposed
Unsure
Unwritten
Unknown Identity Box Set: Books #1-3

Unlucky Series
Unlucky in Love
UnWanted
UnLoved Forever

War Torn Letters Series
My Sweetheart

Wet & Wild Series
Stormy Love
Savage Love
Secure Love

Worth It Series
Worth Billions
Worth Every Cent
Worth More Than Money

You & Me - A Bad Boy Romance
Just Me
Touch Me
Kiss Me

Standalone
Wash
Loving Charity
Summer Lovin'
Love & College
Billionaire Heart
First Love
Frisky and Fun Romance Box Collection
Beating Hades' Bikers

Watch for more at www.lexytimms.com.

My Sweetheart

USA TODAY BESTSELLING AUTHOR
LEXY TIMMS

Copyright 2019

ALL RIGHTS RESERVED. No part of this publication may be reproduced, stored in or introduced into a retrieval system, or transmitted, in any form, or by any means (electronic, mechanical, photocopying, recording, or otherwise) without the prior written permission of both the copyright owner and the above publisher of this book.

This is a work of fiction. Names, characters, places, brands, media, and incidents are either the product of the author's imagination or are used fictitiously. Any resemblance to an actual person, living or dead, events, or locales is entirely coincidental. The author acknowledges the trademarked status and trademark owners of various products referenced in this work of fiction, which have been used without permission. The publication/use of these trademarks is not authorized, associated with, or sponsored by the trademark owners.

All rights reserved.
My Sweetheart – Book 1
War Torn Letter Series
Copyright 2019 by Lexy Timms
Cover by: Book Cover by Design[1]

---

1. http://bookcoverbydesign.co.uk/

War Torn Letter Series

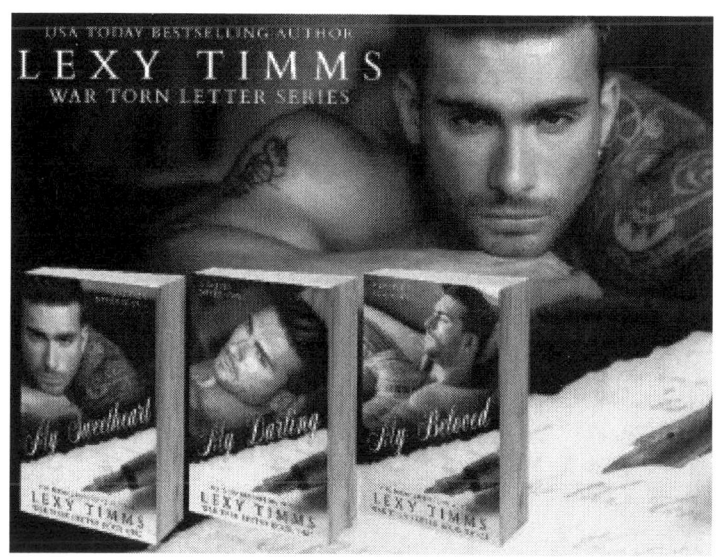

My Sweetheart - Book 1
My Darling - Book 2
My Beloved – Book 3

Find Lexy Timms:

LEXY TIMMS NEWSLETTER:
http://eepurl.com/9i0vD
Lexy Timms Facebook Page:
https://www.facebook.com/SavingForever
Lexy Timms Website:
http://www.lexytimms.com

Want to read more...
For **FREE**?
Sign up for Lexy Timms' newsletter
And she'll send you updates on new releases, ARC copies of books and a whole lotta fun!
Sign up for news and updates!
http://eepurl.com/9i0vD

My Sweetheart Blurb

You have to know the past to understand the present.

IT'S 1942 AND WAR IS raging in Europe and slowly, London is coming undone at the seams. Life as Claire knew it is falling apart all around her. But she's determined to live a full life, to flirt and have fun as if nothing is wrong.

And then she meets Thomas, the handsome American soldier, and with him comes the thrill of secrecy and a whirlwind love that sucks her in. She will wait for him forever, if that's what it takes.

AMELIA JUST STARTED a job at an antique shop at a small town and she love everything that screams nostalgia at her. This is what she escaped the big city for. The slow pace, the taste of a world long gone.

She finds a letter, written by a woman in love a long time ago, and she needs to know how their story ended.

In her attempt to find out what happened, she meets Dane, and a love story of her own unfolds.

Chapter 1

Claire

"Oh, Claire, you made it!" Dorothy squealed when I arrived at The Bell. It was Saturday and despite the weight of the war, London was alive with people who needed to forget. Bright light fell onto the street through the small windows of the pub and I could hear laughter and chatter from inside. Music punctuated the sounds.

"My father will kill me if he finds me on the streets tonight," I said. "But I simply couldn't stay away! Did you watch the parade?"

Dorothy, Margaret, and Ruth all nodded eagerly.

It had been spectacular. It was 1942 and the war had touched London with the finger of death. It hadn't served to demotivate our troops of course—Hitler seemed to think that a few bombings would deter us. But the city had been flattened in many ways and wore the scowl of conflict now.

But the American troops had arrived on Monday to offer a hand in need, and just the other day they had paraded through the streets of London, from Mayfair all the way to the Guildhall. The streets had been lined with spectators. My father and mother had both accompanied me, allowing me to join the crowd and cheer for the soldiers.

The streets had been brimming with energy, with hope and trust that these men would somehow help us overcome the Germans that seemed intent on ruling the world.

"They are so dreamy," Ruth sighed.

"And that is exactly why we are here," I said with a giggle.

MY SWEETHEART

I adjusted my hat, ran my hands down my clothing and glanced at Dorothy.

"Do I look alright?"

Dorothy rolled her eyes at me with dramatic flair. "You don't have the capacity to look anything else. You're a right picture and you know it."

I smiled and shook my head. I wore a midi skirt that reached my calves, and a blouse with wide shoulders that I had tucked into the skirt to accentuate my small waist. My lips were red and I had curled my hair into ringlets that fell over my shoulders. I hoped to speak to one of the foreign soldiers tonight. My friends were all dressed similarly, but I knew that they all looked up to me, that they thought I was more beautiful than they were, as girls were wont to do.

"Let's go inside, it's cold," Ruth said.

We walked toward the pub, the light swallowing us as we walked inside and a few heads turned in our direction. The tang of smoke hung in the air, soaking into my clothing. It hung against the ceiling like an artificial sky. Men and women stood at the bar and in the corner, three couples were dancing to music that streamed from a phonograph. Where had they found one of those?

Smiling, I lifted my chin a little. I knew that men noticed me and I enjoyed the attention I was getting from these men. The soldiers in the bar were not only American, but our men, too. More of them than the Americans, in fact.

I was a little disappointed, but there was still a chance that we would meet some of the Americans. I wanted to drink and dance with them, to get a taste of the exotic.

We walked to a booth toward the back of the pub and a moment later, a waiter arrived to serve us.

"So, did you sneak out?" Ruth asked after we ordered four glasses of beer. There weren't many drinks to choose from these days. Alcohol was scarce with the war.

"I had to," I said. "My father won't let me out on the streets unless he's with me. You know how he can be."

"I understand it," Dorothy said. "Half the city has been flattened and the war is far from over. I wouldn't let a jewel like you walk through the rubble alone, either."

I laughed and shook my head, glancing at the soldiers as I did. A few of them were looking in our direction. And they were dashing in their uniforms, meticulously dressed and ready for action. Would they be our salvation?

"I'm seventeen, Dorothy, I'm sure I'm old enough to make my own decisions."

"They're all staring at you," Ruth said.

I glanced at the men again. A few more of them were looking toward us. But I shook my head.

"They're staring at all of us. Four ladies? I don't blame them, not one bit."

"Don't be modest, Claire," Margaret said. "We all know they're looking at you."

As she said it, the waiter arrived with another round of beers.

"From the gentleman at the bar," he said, putting the glasses in front of us. I looked up and one of the men from the bar lifted a hand at me in a wave. I nodded politely and smiled at him. The attention was flattering. The girls murmured in excited tones.

"How do you do it?" Margaret asked.

"Do what?" I asked innocently.

"She has a face that implores men to lose their minds and dedicate their lives to her," Dorothy said.

"Stop," I laughed.

"If only it was as easy for the rest of us," Ruth said.

"Don't be ridiculous!" I cried out. "We are all of us equally beautiful."

They didn't respond and I was grateful. Sometimes, it frustrated me that my friends put me on a pedestal. I knew that I had the sort of face that drew attention. But there were days when I wished it wasn't so. Sometimes, I wished that I would be noticed for what I had to offer, rather than how beautiful I would look on someone's arm. One day, my father would expect me to take a husband. And how would I find someone who truly loved me for who I was if he was so taken by my appearance?

"Hello ladies," a soldier said, walking up to our table. He wore the British uniform and his accent was very much like ours.

I noticed the disappointment on my friends' faces. We were here for the foreigners. We could meet locals at any time, but it wasn't every day that the Americans were here to assist us with the war.

"Ladies like you shouldn't be in a place like this," he said.

"We are quite comfortable, thank you," I said tightly.

He smiled at me. He had kind eyes and a small scar on his cheek. He was handsome. And noble, fighting for the cause. But he wasn't a man to draw my attention.

The girls struck up a conversation with the soldier and I turned my attention back to the men. Americans were clustered at the bar in the one corner, keeping to themselves. They spoke quietly and drank their beers in peace. They didn't seem to feel comfortable around our people.

After a short while, the local soldier moved on.

"Thank you, Claire," Margaret said bitterly.

"What?" I asked.

"You could have pretended to be interested, so that he would stay and talk, at least."

"Don't blame me that he left," I said, shrugging off the accusation. There was movement at the door and five Americans walked in, their uniforms distinct. They glanced around the room and one of them noticed me, eyes resting on my face for a moment.

He was the most handsome man I had ever seen— tall, dark, and handsome. The perfect combination, as if he had stepped from the pages of a novel. His face was carved by the angels themselves. An Adonis. His dark eyes burrowed into mine and I wanted to meet him.

"Oh, they're all so handsome!" Ruth said, leaning forward a little.

We stared shamelessly at the soldiers as they walked to the bar. I watched him lean on the bar, his confidence spilling outward and filling the corners of the room. Everyone else faded away and it was as if he was alone, the only other person in the bar aside from myself.

They ordered beers and started talking. And I waited. I wanted the tall, muscular soldier with the dark eyes to come to me, to offer to buy me a drink, perhaps ask me to dance.

But he didn't. He didn't even glance in my direction again. And it offended me.

I was the girl everyone noticed. But he pretended like I didn't exist, he drank as if he was here on business alone, and disregarded pleasure completely.

"Can you believe they're just staying there?" I asked.

Ruth frowned at me. "They arrived not five minutes ago."

I didn't answer her. She was right, of course. But I wanted them to acknowledge us. I wanted their attention. His attention, in particular.

"They have plenty of time to join us," I said.

Dorothy laughed at my tone. "I can't believe you're getting angry that they're not noticing you! It seems as though Claire Whiteside can be overlooked, after all."

"It's not necessary to be rude about it," I snapped at Dorothy, who snapped her mouth shut. But she was right, of course. Not all men had to stare at me in awe and wonder. And it was spoiled of me to expect it.

But if there was ever a man I wanted to notice me, to swoon over me and trip over his own feet, it would be this one. The one man who didn't do it.

MY SWEETHEART

Which only made me determined to get his attention. There was something about having what you weren't allowed to have that had always appealed to me. The excitement, the danger. Breaking the rules.

It was, after all, why I had snuck out of the house to come to the pub at ten in the evening when my father had forbade me from walking in the streets of London without a chaperone. It was why I was here, dressed up and ready to accept attention, when I knew my father would skin me alive if he found out I was ready to flirt with the foreigners.

And it was why I was more than ready to reject any local men that tried to pay attention to me. Because that wasn't what I wanted.

"Which one is it?" Ruth asked, when I glanced toward the bar again.

"The tall one," I said. "With the stark expression."

"He really is handsome," Ruth said.

I nodded. He was more than handsome. But he was also drinking and talking to his friends without paying attention to us at all.

"Perhaps we should go home soon," Margaret said.

I glared at her. "Why?"

"Because it's getting late and I have a curfew. We all don't get to break the rules, Claire."

I shook my head. "You're welcome to leave if you'd rather, but I'm not going with you."

"It would only look like you're asking for attention, and that won't go down well," Dorothy said. "You can't stay here alone."

I shook my head and slid out of the booth. I ran my hands down my skirt and touched my hair.

"I won't be alone," I said.

"Where are you going?" Ruth asked.

I turned to the girls.

"I'm going to make sure he notices me."

They all looked shocked, but my mind was made up. If Adonis wasn't going to notice me, I would put myself in his line of vision. If he wasn't going to come to speak to me, I would strike up the conversation.

"That's very untoward," Ruth said.

"Yes, I believe it is," I said. "But you won't stop me. We're in the middle of a war, girls. We're lucky we're even still alive. Who knows what tomorrow will bring? If this is going to be my last night, I'm going to get what I want."

"No one is dying tomorrow," Margaret said, rolling her eyes. "You're so dramatic."

I smiled. "I know," I said, and walked to the bar.

Chapter 2

Thomas

London was beautiful. It was stark and gray compared to the green rolling hills of Montana, where my family ranch lay basking in the morning sun. But London had its only appeal. It was like a businessman at the end of a long day, who was yet to loosen his tie and undo the top button of his shirt.

But the war had not been kind to the city. There was rubble in the streets, and the signs of loss etched on the faces of the people I passed every day. There was also determination, though. Whatever Hitler had been playing at when he had started The Blitz, raining bombs on England to break their spirit, it hadn't worked. They were going to get through this mighty fine.

And we were here to help. We were going to kick Hitler's ass.

Since we had arrived in London, we had been training. They had briefed us on everything we needed to know. And soon, we were going to be deployed to the front. It was Saturday and it was the last night we had to have a bit of fun. Judging by how things looked in the rest of Europe, it would be the last bit of fun in quite a while.

And I was eager to get out on the town, to see what London's night life had to offer, to see the smiles on faces that had only learned how to frown over the past two years.

"Ready, Thomas?" Harry asked. "The boys are waiting."

I ran the comb through my hair one more time and nodded, turning away from the little mirror.

"Ready," I said.

"If we're lucky, we can find us a couple of dames," Harry said.

I shook my head. "I'm not here to spend my night with a woman. Besides, we leave soon, and then what will be leave behind?"

"You're too good, Thomas," Harry said. "I wasn't planning on even remembering her name. Foreign soil, man. And who knows what will happen once we head out there. Live hard while you can."

I chuckled and shook my head. Harry and the rest of the boys all had their minds on sex. But I wasn't here for anything like that. I wanted to enjoy myself, see a bit of the city, and get my mind clear so that by the time we headed out, I knew where I was headed. I wanted a chance to breathe before we would have to lay our lives on the line for a country that wasn't our own.

The Bell was a British pub in the true sense of the word, with low ceilings, a dark interior, and food on the menu I had never heard of. We walked toward the door and I felt eyes on me. When I looked over my shoulder, four women were watching us.

Emerald green eyes pierced my heart.

But I wasn't here to find a woman, I told myself. And I followed Harry to the bar.

We drank. We talked. We laughed. The British were so different and we talked about it without trying to be too loud, so that the others around us—the British soldiers —would hear us, too.

"Excuse me," a woman said, and the men all stopped talking. I turned and realized she was looking at me. She had a beer in her hand and held it out to me.

I took it from her, shocked.

"Did you buy me a drink?" I asked.

She nodded and held out her hand. "I'm Claire."

It was the dark haired beauty I had noticed at the booth when I first came in. She was drop dead gorgeous from up close. I hadn't planned to drink a lot. I hadn't planned to have more than one beer. But she was so arrogant, so confident, walking up to a group of men and offering me a beer.

I had never seen anyone more beautiful in my life. Her skin was flawless, her lips a bright red and her eyes were seafoam green, pools that I could drown in.

"Thomas," I said, and took her hand. She was delicate, her waist tiny, her arms slender. But there was a fire in her eyes. This woman was silk over steel.

And I wanted to know her.

Harry cleared his throat and I remembered that I wasn't alone in the bar.

"This is Harry," I said, clapping him on the back. "And Paul, Andrew, Mark, and Howard." I rattled through the others. "You're not with your friends?"

Claire glanced over her shoulder at her friends, who looked at us with excited smiles.

"They were about ready to leave," she said.

"Not if we can help it," Harry said, and marched over there with the two guys in tow. I laughed and looked back at Claire.

"It was very forward of you to bring me a beer," I said.

"Sometimes you need to fight for what you want."

I raised my eyebrows. "You need to know what you want, first."

"Absolutely," Claire said with a curt nod.

I had never met someone like her before. She was so determined, so headstrong. And she wasn't shy at all. I would never have imagined a woman coming up to me the way she had. And with a beer, too. I was drawn to her in a way I couldn't explain. I had the terrible urge to touch her cheek, to run my fingertips down her flawless skin.

"Shall we dance?" I asked, instead.

Claire nodded, a smile spreading across her features, and it was beautiful, lighting up the world like a sunrise after the darkest of nights.

I held out my hand and she took it. Her hand was small in mine, her fingers slim and I relished the feel of her skin on mine. We moved across the pub and joined the couples that were dancing.

And it felt like I was being transported. I slipped my hand around her waist, and she looked up at me with eyes that promised sights of a world I had never known. And everything else fell away. I forgot why I was here. I forgot about the war and about fighting for the greater good. I forgot about my promise that this wouldn't be about a woman.

All I could see were her eyes, pools of greens with golden flecks that danced when she laughed, and a smile that swept me off my feet.

I didn't know how long we danced, but by the time we stepped off the dance floor to ask the barman for a glass of water, the bar had emptied significantly.

"Do you want to get out of here?" Claire asked me.

I eyed her. What did she have in mind? She was a classy lady and she didn't seem like the type to just take a man home. But I wasn't sure, it was so difficult to know what their intentions were in these modern times.

She laughed when I didn't respond. "I didn't mean for it to come across the wrong way. I meant to leave the pub and find something that will distract us. Sometimes, I feel like I can't breathe within these four walls that close in around me. My life isn't always as free as I'd like for it to be."

I had grown up wild and free, literally, on my parents' ranch. But being here in London, I could imagine how someone could be stifled. Especially someone as beautiful and young as Claire. She couldn't be eighteen yet, if I had to guess.

"Let's," I agreed, deciding to put my trust in her hands. She was different than anyone I had met before, and I was willing to see where the night would lead us.

We left the bar together. I noticed that her friends had all left already. And mine were gone, too. They had all returned to the base. I was breaking curfew. I was breaking many rules to go with Claire.

But I didn't care. Meeting someone like her only happened once in a lifetime and I wasn't going to let this opportunity slip through my fingers. We were in the middle of a war that was far from over. What if something like this never happened again?

It was strange to be deployed to fight for a country. Your days suddenly changed, you started to think in the moment, because any moment could end up being your last.

Claire took my hand and I followed her. We walked through the dark streets. It could have been dangerous. She was taking a risk being outside at night at all, I guessed. We walked through remains of the bombings that had happened in the past year or two, the scars that war left on any town.

And I looked at Claire and when she looked over her shoulder back at me, I saw nothing of the death and destruction. Instead, I saw the light in her eyes, a light that felt like it was guiding me home.

She showed me London the way I would have seen it, had I come as a tourist. She showed me the Big Ben, the Tower of London, and we passed the palace. She explained to me that the princesses had been hidden away in case something went wrong, but that the King remained steadfast.

But the truth was I heard very little of what she explained to me. I saw a city that held its heritage in the palm of its hand like a jewel, I saw a place that Claire was proud of in a way I had never been proud of my country. But I was mesmerized by her lips when she talked. I wanted to kiss her every time she said something interesting.

Which was all the time.

I didn't realize how the time passed as we walked the streets together. Dawn wasn't far off, the horizon already colored with the silver announcement of its coming. The lights still shone in the streets but the sky had lost its inky quality and it was the start of a new day.

She huddled against me, her coat crossed over her chest and I put my arm around her shoulders to shield her from the cold. Her hair smelled like what I imagined heaven to smell like.

"This is it," she breathed. "Westminster Abbey."

I looked up at a church that towered over us in the darkness, built with care and intricacy. The windows were taped and covered and the damage of the bombs could be seen here and there, the shadows catching in the dim light from the streets.

"Can you imagine it?" she asked, in a voice that was distant, as if she was talking to herself rather than to me. "Centuries are held within these walls. It stood the test of time. And even if they tried to bomb it now, it wouldn't go down. This is what we're like you know."

She finally turned her face to me. "This is what the United Kingdom is like. An injured soldier is not dead yet."

I fell into her eyes, drowned by her passion and determination. This was why the war would not be won by those who wanted to cease control of the world. Because there were nations who vowed to never give up.

The sun crept over the horizon, the rays falling on her face, and in that moment I was sure that she was heaven sent, that this wasn't a girl but an angel who must have lost her way.

"I have to go," she said, with words that shattered me. I had hoped, believed, that this could last forever.

"When can I see you again?" I asked. I had to see her. I couldn't go to war and not know that this girl could somehow be mine.

"I don't know," she said. Her eyes slid to the left before she looked at me again. "Tuesday. At The Bell, at nine. Meet me there."

I nodded. "I'll be there."

"Don't be late," she said.

I wouldn't miss it for the world. But I didn't say that to her. I didn't tell her anything in words. I grabbed her, and I kissed her. I had been aching to do it all night. She melted against me when our lips pressed together and everything around us fell away. I wasn't an American soldier fighting in a war that was not my own. And she wasn't a British girl with a dangerous beauty and something about her that couldn't be tamed.

We were two people that fate had thrown together because it was just how it should be.

She broke the kiss and took a step back, with longing in her eyes.

"Tuesday," she whispered, then turned around and skipped away.

I stood alone in front of Westminster Abbey. It looked like a jewel in the morning sun, despite how it had been prepared for war, despite how it had been damaged. And I knew that no matter what happened from here on out, that even if this was my last moment, I would die a happy man.

Pinewood, Oklahoma – Present Day

Chapter 3

Dane

Roses were full of shit, if you wanted to know the truth. They needed more attention than any woman I had met and they picked up diseases in a snap, getting sick faster than a toddler. I had always wondered why anyone would waste their time looking after flowers that were a hell of a mission for most of the year and died the moment you picked them.

Let alone the romantic implications. If any man upset his woman, roses would do the trick. Valentine's Day, birthdays, anniversaries and surprises—it was a lot of pressure for a flower that didn't know how to exist without human intervention nine months out of the year.

But these roses had saved my damn life. PTSD was a bitch and trimming the roses, spraying them with whatever meds my gran told me to give them, and making sure that they were worth looking at, was exactly the thing that stopped me from losing my mind.

So, I sat like some proud gardener, trimming the leaves from one of the white rose bushes and thinking about that stupid Alice in Wonderland song where the cards were painting the roses red.

My gran's estate was large, and she kept it the way the British estates were kept, with the classic English gardening style. Sometimes, I wondered why my Grandma Claire didn't go back to London now that my gramps had passed away. She spoke of it so often these days.

But she was happy here, she said. It was where her heart lay. And no one was going to argue with her. She was the most stubborn person this side of the Atlantic.

I stood after finishing the rose bush and pressed my hands to my back until it clicked. I rotated my shoulder, wincing when it ached in the socket where they had dug out two bullets. It was going to take a while before I could use this bad boy again. And until then, I was off duty.

Fine by me. I still struggled with nightmares sometimes, where I felt like my life was stuffed into the barrel of a gun.

I turned around and looked out over the estate gardens. They were beautiful. My gran had designed the whole thing, and my gramps had made it happen for her. On the days where I wasn't out here with my fingers in the ground, a team of skilled gardeners maintained this place to look as fancy as the Queen of England herself.

The truth was, even though I had a lot of shitty things to say about roses and the idea of throwing your life away gardening, I loved it here. It was beautiful. And lately I had been feeling like beauty was a rare thing to come by. And the gardens were peaceful, too. Heavens knew I needed peaceful in my life after the shooting.

Just thinking about it had me breaking out in a cold sweat. At least I didn't have to sit down, put my head between my knees and focus on breathing anymore. There had been a time, just after I had been taken down with two other officers, where I had been terrified. Where I had woken up in the middle of the night, feeling like I was choking on bullets, feeling like my lungs were being ripped out of my chest.

Rose bushes were lined up in a pattern that looked almost like a maze, with hedges that needed to be trimmed beyond that, before you reached the house. And the roses were all red and white. I wondered why. My gran was famous for her roses. She could cultivate so many colors. But she refused to grow anything other than red and white.

After I used the hose to water the rose bushes I had trimmed, I left it for one of the gardeners to continue, I pulled off the gloves and dumped them next to the hose pipe. I wiped my hands on my jeans as if they were still filthy, and walked toward the house. I wiped my brow. I was sweating like a pig after being in the sun.

A pig. Ha. That was funny since I was a cop. If I was still a cop after the shooting. No, I shook my head. My therapist had told me that I couldn't think like this. I had to stay positive about my worth.

"There you are," my gran said. "You're red in the face! Splash some water on your face, and then join me on the veranda for lemonade." She had been here for decades now, and her British accent was still perfect. I had always loved that about her as a kid. It had been nothing like the thick, rolling accent my gramps used to speak with.

"I'll be right out, Nana" I said.

My grandma Claire was the classiest woman I had ever seen, and that I would ever see, I was certain. She carried herself with elegance and grace. Her white hair was always coiffed neatly. She refused to get it cut into the short, modern haircuts old ladies liked these days. And she wore dress suits with blouses and two inch heels.

Even if she wasn't going anywhere or expecting anyone. It like she still always dressed up for my gramps. Even though he had been gone for a while now.

I did as she had told me, splashing my face with water. If I didn't do it, she would berate me. And I wasn't going to fight with her.

When I walked outside, I found her seated on one of the wicker chairs. She poured two glasses of lemonade when I sat down and took one. I took the other and sipped it. It was tart, as always. My gran didn't believe in sweet lemonade. She used the recipe her mom had used since she'd been a kid.

And I didn't fight it, even though I would have preferred 7-Up from the store or something. Because you didn't throw homemade lemonade into someone like my Grandma Claire's face.

"How are you, Dane?" she asked. Her green eyes were sharp and they bored into mine.

"I'm doing better," I said. I had always believed she would know if I was lying.

She nodded. "You do look better. Time heals all wounds, doesn't it?"

I nodded. "Time is all we need."

She turned her face to the garden. "Most of the time."

I frowned, and I wanted to ask. But Grandma Claire wouldn't talk about anything that bothered her unless she wanted to. Asking would only get a brush-off answer if the timing wasn't right. And my timing was pretty shit with pretty much everything lately.

"I'm not the woman I used to be, Dane," she said, after a while. "I'm getting old. Sometimes I feel like the world I know is slipping away from me."

I didn't know what to say. She had always been the same to me, elegant and collected, cool in any situation. But I hadn't know the person she had been before she had come home with gramps, when she had still been the woman living in the UK. But she was becoming more and more unhappy. That I had noticed.

And I wished I could make it better, somehow. I guess that was what happened when you lost your other half.

"Do you miss him?" I asked.

She looked at me with a slight frown. I wondered if it was wrong of me to ask.

"Your grandfather?" she asked. She put her glass down on the small side table next to her, the contents barely touched.

I nodded. Who else could I have been talking about? My gran looked at me for the longest time before she turned her head back to the gardens we looked out over.

"I miss the company. The laughter in the house, the movement between these walls. The sound of the television with his sports and the tea he brought me in the mornings."

MY SWEETHEART

I stayed silent, waiting for her to tell me more. I had never had someone that meant so much to me. I had never understood what it felt like to have the other half of me ripped away. But when I looked at my gran, I tried to imagine what it had to have been like. To leave your home, your country, to go to a new world because you loved someone that much.

I tried to think what it could be like to give up so much for someone, to give up everything that mattered. My gran had done that for my gramps. She had done that because she had given him her heart, and everything else had followed. I wanted her to tell me that she missed him.

Because even though I didn't believe that love like that existed anymore, or that I would ever find it, I knew that it had been real for my gran. She was here, after all. She had followed her husband across the sea.

But she didn't say it. She didn't tell me how much she missed my gramps, or that she was incomplete without him.

"Aside from the routine, though," I said, pressing on. "Do you miss him?"

My gran sighed and glanced at me again with an expression I didn't understand. She reached for her lemonade glass and brought it to her lips, trembling. She took a sip and put it down again, staring out at the gardens.

I didn't ask questions. I knew better than to challenge my gran. She was a lady that you respected. But I wondered why she wouldn't answer me. I wondered how it was possible to lose so much, to become so unhappy without someone, and to keep it all inside.

But my gran had never spoken about her feelings much. It wasn't in her nature.

I sat back, balancing my lemonade on my thigh, and looked out at the gardens, too.

Maybe it was good that love like that didn't exist anymore. It was a shame that I would never experience it. But it was good to know that it could never be ripped away, either.

I had enough pain and suffering to work through without adding a broken heart or something like that to the list.

Chapter 4

Amelia

Everybody complained about Mondays, but I liked them. I liked getting back to work, getting my week going again after the weekend.

But that was because my job at Pinewood Antiques was amazing. I loved it here, surrounded by the nostalgia that came in with the old objects people brought in or bought. Knowing that someone had cherished the items we sold, that it had a history, that it had stood the test of time, made me giddy with excitement.

There was something about the past and the present connecting that excited me.

"Amelia," Arthur said, popping his head out from the backroom. His gray hair was disheveled and his glasses were on his head, not his nose. "Come look at this."

I left the counter and walked to the back room, curious. When I pushed the door open, Arthur stood in the middle of the room, surrounded by the shelves of boxes and antiques that were either too broken or too precious to sell. In here, he looked at home. The magician in his room of magic. He had hands on his hips, admiring a music box that stood on the table.

"Oh, my goodness," I breathed, taking a step closer, moving carefully as if I could scare the delicate item away. "Does it work?"

Arthur nodded and carefully opened the lid. A small figurine popped up and slowly started turning as music played. The box was carved with an intricate design, dust thick in the small corners. The figure had been carved from ivory, it seemed. And the music was a tune I didn't recognize.

"It's German. Sixteen hundreds, if you ask me. I'll get it checked out to see for sure. This is a real gem." He looked at me with sparkling eyes. I had never seen anyone as excited about history as this man and it was a pleasure to work with him. Every day was like a journey to discover treasures from life long gone.

"You can't sell this here," I said. "It's far too valuable. We don't have anything older than a couple of decades."

"I know," Arthur breathed.

"Where did you get it?"

Arthur pointed at a box. "Someone brought it in yesterday, saying they wanted just a few dollars for the whole thing."

"If only they knew," I said.

We stood together in silence for a while, staring at the music box. I couldn't believe it. Once in a while, gems like these appeared. Everything in the shop was fantastic, but these little treasures were spectacular. A while ago, Arthur had found a sugar spoon collection that was also as valuable as I imagined this would be.

Arthur turned to me, snapping out of his reverie.

"I'm leaving in a short while," he said. "You'll be fine without me?"

I nodded. "More than fine."

Arthur nodded, satisfied with my answer. "I'm expecting an online order sometime this week. You'll take care of it?"

"Of course," I said. I had signed for deliveries before. I loved unpacking the new stuff, logging it into the inventory system and putting it on display.

"You're a life saver, Amelia," Arthur said and squeezed my hand. "I don't know what I would do without you."

"Nerd out about these things alone," I said with a grin.

Arthur laughed and nodded. "You bet. If I had enough cash coming in, you know I'd give you a raise."

I laughed. "I'm more than happy with everything I have here, Arthur. Now, get going. You don't want to miss your flight."

Arthur checked his watch and walked to the door. He turned before leaving the room. "I'll just be a week."

I giggled. "I'll be fine, Arthur. I'll phone and check in."

Arthur smiled at me and left the back room. I turned back to the music box and sighed, sinking onto my heels to look at it from every angle. The craftsmanship was fantastic. It had be hand carved. So much effort and attention to detail had gone into it. I wondered who had made it. And for whom. I imagined it was a carpenter who made something like this in his spare time for his daughter. Or for his lover.

Or a famous designer who created it for nobility, as a gift or tribute.

I had to get back to the front of the shop. I carefully closed the music box and put it on one of the shelves, handling it carefully.

The shop was lined with shelves against the walls, and small tables in the middle that all showcased the antiques we sold. The lighting was dim, creating a cozy atmosphere, and the colors were neutral where we had managed to sneak in some kind of décor. The items and objects we sold were really what it was about, though.

We had a large variety of things. Silver children's hair brushes that dated back to the twenties. Records that had survived the sixties and seventies.

Jewelry that was made in a Victorian style.

I walked through the shelves and adjusted some of the pieces, making sure everything was dusted and clean. I knew everything about every piece. I loved looking it up, finding out where it came from, when it had been made. If possible, I wanted to know who had owned it.

The bell above the door rang and a young woman walked in. I smiled at her.

"Good morning," I said. "Can I help you with anything?"

She shook her head. "No, I'm just going to take a look around."

"Please," I said, and waited by the counter in case she needed me.

It wasn't long before she stopped in front of a vintage typewriter.

"Did this belong to someone famous?" she asked.

I stepped closer. "Unfortunately not," I said. "But there is a great story behind it. An old man brought it in about a month ago. When I bought it from him, I asked him where it had come from. I love knowing these things about the items in the shop. He told me it had belonged to his mother, who had used it to write advice columns for a local newspaper."

"Really?" the woman asked.

"Yeah, I have some of the columns, too. He brought it in about a week later." I walked back to the counter and found the scrapbook the older gentleman had brought in. I walked with it to the customer and opened the book. It contained old newspaper clippings of several different things, including the Aunt Agony column.

"This is amazing," she said, reading through the information. "Dear Aunt Edith." She looked at me. "How do people get into something like this?"

"Well, he told me that his dad had passed when he'd been just a baby. A truck hit his bicycle."

"Oh, no."

"She needed money to take care of three children, her teaching post didn't earn enough. It's amazing what we will do when it's needed, isn't it?"

She nodded, running her fingers over the typewriter. "I'll take it. Could I—would it be possible to buy the column pieces as well?"

"Of course, it's exactly why I kept them."

We walked to the counter with the type writer and the book. Carefully, I took out the laminated pages with the column pieces and I rang up the typewriter and all its affects. When the customer left, I sighed. It was always hard to part with the history and the memories that came with the items. But at the same time, the sale made me happy. Being able to share stories of the past was amazing.

MY SWEETHEART

We were storytellers, after all. This was human nature, holding onto the past and letting it shape our futures.

The doorbell rang again and a man walked in. He wore a business suit and he was graying at the temples, with a moustache on his lip and a frown on his face.

"I don't recognize you," he said. "Are you new?"

"I've been working here for about a month," I said. "And you are—"

"Owen. Craig Owen."

"Amelia," I said, and held out my hand. He took it and squeezed hard. This was a brusque man. He was handsome, but his manner was abrupt and borderline offensive. Still, he was customer.

"I often come here when I'm in town. Are you new in the area?"

I nodded. "I moved to Pinetown just over a month ago. I started working here almost immediately." I stood behind the counter and flattened my hands on it, trying to stay engaged in the conversation. I wasn't sure why he was so chatty, but small talk was the name of the game in any retail position.

"Where did you move from?" he asked.

"New York," I said.

Owen raised his eyebrows. "Do you have family here?"

I shook my head.

"Then why would you come to such a small town?"

I pulled up my shoulders. "I needed a change of pace. It's easy to work so hard and keep running that you don't stop to realize who you are anymore."

Owen nodded. "That I can understand. Well, if a slower pace is what you're looking for, then Pinetown is the place for you. Nothing ever happens here. And I really do mean, nothing."

I chuckled. "That suits me just fine."

I had been a Personal Assistant in the city, so busy arranging someone else's life that I hadn't realized I didn't have one anymore. And when I tried to figure out what I wanted to do instead, all I could think of was getting away.

So I left and moved here. I had read about it, and it was as good a place as any to escape to. The move had been the best thing I'd ever done.

"The community here is so accepting and inviting," I said. "I've felt very welcome from day one."

Owen nodded. "Yes, it is like a big family here, with everyone knowing everyone else."

"That's exactly it," I said, thinking about how Mrs. Kelley at the bakery had given me free baguettes on the first day, and how Keith from the locksmith hadn't only changed my locks when I'd moved in, but he'd also told me that the convenience store restocked their shelves on Wednesdays if I wanted to get the best stuff. And Beth, a barista at the coffee shop next door, had acted like I was a long lost sister.

"The problem is that everyone is as involved in your life as family is, too. You can never keep secrets around here, Amelia."

"It's a good thing I don't have anything to hide, then," I said with a smile that didn't reach my eyes. I had learned this expression when I had worked as a PA.

Owen nodded without saying anything else.

"Is there anything I can help with?" I asked.

"I was looking for Arthur, actually," he said.

"He just left for the week," I said, relieved that I didn't have to keep talking to this man about my life. Something about the way he talked to me about the choices I'd made seemed condescending.

"Oh, pity," Owen said. "Well, it was nice meeting you, Amelia."

"Likewise," I said, and smiled again.

Owen nodded at me and turned on his heel, walking out of the shop as abruptly as he'd come in. I leaned on the counter with my elbows. Now that he'd brought it up again, I thought about New York. I hadn't thought about my life back there since the moment I had arrived. I was just so happy here. The small town life worked for me so far. I liked the people, I loved my job, and I was able to just be. This kind of life, so carefree and quiet, was what I'd always wanted.

And even if Craig Owen seemed to think I was a fool to give up a life in New York, I was happier now than I had ever been. I was fulfilled, I didn't need anyone or anything beyond what I already had.

This was a good fit for me.

Chapter 5

Claire

We sat at the breakfast table. The sun fell in through the French windows and the room was warm. A servant brought in a warm pot of tea, pouring for each of us before setting it down on the table.

My father read the paper, leaning back in his seat, his waistcoat buttoned up and his ankle throw over his knee. My mother stared in deep contemplation at the opposite wall while she chewed, her slim fingers holding a piece of toast with marmalade. She had eaten the same thing every morning since I could remember.

I sliced my fruit in silence. We never made much conversation at breakfast. Come to think of it, we never made much conversation in general. If there was anything spoken, it was my father who offered his opinion. And my mother and I agreed with him more often than we disagreed, simply to avoid friction.

Another servant arrived with the plate of pork sausage my father had requested specifically.

Despite the war, and various products becoming scarcer, my father still pulled strings to receive what we needed. And more. Where other families, even those in our very own street, had to make do without sugar or butter, we still had plenty of each. I didn't quite understand my father's intent of living as if nothing had changed. The world was swiftly becoming a charred edition of what it had once been. But my father liked to pretend that we were not affected by the war around us.

My father created the world we existed in, and insisted that it was a good world.

My father was well-off, with connections in high places and he was highly respected by everyone in his circles. He had been in a position of power at the bank before the war had started, and even though he was home a lot more often now, with the war affecting every career in England, he still carried his illusions of grandeur with him wherever he went.

And my mother and I reaped the benefits of it.

Or we suffered the consequences of living under his rule. Some said we were lucky to have to sacrifice so little when there were others that had lost so much. But there were times where I wondered what the price was for freedom.

"It looks like things are going well," my father said, speaking out loud assuming we would want to hear what he had to say. "The war is raging on, but with the Americans here, we're sure to make headway." He folded the paper. "We should not have been involved in this war in the first place, should we? If you ask me, Hitler is looking for trouble in places where he might very well find it."

None of us had asked him, but I knew better than to voice my opinion. My father was not in the habit of listening to the opinion of a woman.

I cleared my throat. "May I visit Ruth today?" I asked. "Her family has asked me over for supper tonight."

My father and mother both looked at me.

"Strange time to host dinner parties, isn't it?" my father said. "There is a war raging outside, or hadn't they noticed?" The irony was glaring when my father refused to make do without any luxuries. Although, he had stopped hosting dinner parties, I had to admit.

"Life must continue, Henry," my mother said softly. "We can't all put our lives on hold in fear of another bomb dropping on our heads."

"So, can I go?" I asked.

It would be easier to sneak out of Ruth's house to see Thomas. Ruth had invited me after we had talked about it, after I had told her that it would be better that way. She was always on my side. All my friends were. But her parents hadn't invited me to dinner. That had been a fib.

My father shook his head. "It's too dangerous."

"I will be indoors," I protested. I fiddled with the hem of the white table cloth in my lap. I was taking a risk contradicting my father. But his mood wasn't as dangerous as it could sometimes be. "And I will be as safe as I am here. Mr. Allen is very serious about Ruth's safety, as serious as you are about mine, father."

My father looked at me with a stern expression.

"You see, my darling," he said in a tone that negated the endearment. "I don't believe you will remain indoors. Having you in the same room as any of your friends only poses difficulties we don't need at the moment."

"They're only children, dear," my mother said. Her fingers were curled around the silver fork in her hand, but it rested on the place. She was nervous to voice her opinion, more nervous than I was.

"No, Agatha. They're young ladies. And they need to assume responsibility for their lives at some point or another." My father was yet to raise his voice, but my mother flinched lightly, anyway.

I wanted to say that it wasn't possible if my father always kept me indoors. How could I learn to fend for myself if my father wouldn't allow me to do anything? But I didn't say a word about it. I knew when to speak, and when not to.

"Perhaps a dinner with the Allen's won't hurt," my mother said. She was standing up for me, bless her soul. She could get in trouble for it.

"I said no, Agatha." His voice was sharp and my mother turned her face away. "And that's final." He looked at me. "Don't think I don't know about your little gallivant on Saturday night."

My body went cold. How had he found out? I had returned to my room well before my mother had come to bid me good morning.

"I don't trust that you won't do something so foolish again."

"But father—"

"No. You will not contradict me again, Claire. The streets of London are no place for a lady, especially not at night."

"We don't know that there won't be another airstrike or more bombs anytime soon. We could die right here. Even if we stay indoors for the remainder of the war, we still might not survive."

"That's only half of the problem," my father said. "The streets are littered with vagabonds, people who have lost hope, and their morals along with it. War changes people, Claire. And they turn into monsters. Besides, the Americans are everywhere and they cannot be trusted."

I glanced at my mother, but she kept her eyes averted. She wasn't going to get involved again. My father had berated her enough times in her lifetime that she was subdued now, unwilling to stand up to him. She was the perfect wife in his eyes because she never spoke up.

"You said just a moment ago that the Americans might make a difference in the war." I was losing this battle. I wasn't going to be able to go to Ruth and I was starting to panic.

"On the battlefield, they are our allies and I am grateful that we have help," my father said. "But they are vulgar people. And until they leave, I want you far away from them."

I flashed on Thomas's face, his deep eyes. I thought about the way he had kissed me, as if there would be no tomorrow, and my stomach tightened, warmth rushing through my body.

"As soon as they leave for deployment, we can revise your social calendar."

It was my father's way of bending. He was willing to give me what I wanted within reason. It was just a pity he had no idea what I wanted. Disappointment tugged at me and my mood sank. If I couldn't go to Ruth, I couldn't meet Thomas. And I wanted to see him. Desperately.

"May I be excused?" I asked. I had lost my appetite.

"You may," my father said, opening the paper with a flick.

I stood from the table. My mother looked at me, but I didn't make eye contact. She wouldn't make an effort to stand up against my father. She had faltered the moment he addressed her sternly. She was not on my side and she never would be. I turned and walked to my room. I closed the door before I let my face crumple and I dropped myself on the bed.

Oh, the agony. I felt like I couldn't breathe. My ears were hot, my mind racing. How was I going to see Thomas again? I couldn't let him slip away from me. I couldn't stand the thought of him going to war without me seeing him again. Who knew what would happen once he left, and if he was to die, I was certain my life would be over.

Because I loved him. I could feel it in my bones.

It was absolutely ridiculous, I knew that. I was seventeen and I didn't even know what love was. Wasn't that what the adults always told girls like me? My heart had never been broken, I had never given myself to a man. Someone else had never filled my heart.

But when I had been with him, it was as though Thomas had been lost at sea for the duration of my life, and had finally come home. Being in his arms had felt as though I belonged there all along. And parting from him had brought incredible sorrow, as if I was leaving a piece of my soul behind.

I wasn't being melodramatic. I knew that my heart belonged with his. I had read so many stories about love, about what it meant to find that one person you couldn't bear to live without. Had Mr. Darcy not asked Elizabeth Bennet to marry him mere weeks after meeting her? Because he had known. And what of Jane Eyre and Rochester?

And yes, it was true, these characters were all in fiction. But nothing was written that did not exist in our world.

And I believed that I had met my Sir Galahad. I didn't care that the world would disagree with me, and call me mad. When I thought of him, I felt as though I was made of air, as though I would float away. I knew what I felt.

And I knew that I had to see him again.

My father feared that I would be snatched up by someone, that I would be stolen away. That was what he always said. But the truth was, he feared losing control over my life. He was worried that one day I would belong to someone else and his say wouldn't matter anymore.

So he would hold onto me as long as he could, choosing who I belonged with so that he could decide what became of me. But I wasn't a possession. I had a mind of my own, a heart that yearned for a life that my father would never want for me.

I wasn't going to stay indoors tonight for the sake of my father's need to reign over this household with an iron fist. I was going to see Thomas. My agony turned into determination, and the panic faded.

After my mother came to say goodnight, I dressed myself. I moved quietly, not daring to switch on a light for fear of waking my parents. My hands trembled as I buttoned my clothes, and I strained my ears for sounds in the house. But my parents were early risers and went to bed soon after supper. And as long as I stayed silent, they wouldn't hear me.

My nerves were raw. I was terrified I would be caught, and stopped.

When I was dressed in boots and a skirt, with a warm coat against the chill of the night, I opened my window. It creaked and I felt like the sound had sliced through my body. I froze and listened, but I heard no sound in the house. It was very unladylike of me to sneak out through the window, my father would be shocked.

But he would be far unhappier if he knew where I was going.

Quietly, I crept through the garden. Out here, I could breathe easier, and I was almost free of the confines of my father's reign. Everything looked like it had been painted by a silver brush, muting the daylight colors. The light of the moon was bright enough to see by.

As soon as I was in the road, the cobbles sure beneath my feet, I walked faster. My heart felt as if it was going to burst from my chest, and excitement fueled me now that I had succeeded to escape. Eventually, I broke into a run.

We lived some distance away from The Bell, in a rich neighborhood, but I made the entire journey on foot. I couldn't afford to take a taxi and there were few people out at night. As long as I hurried, I would be safe.

It felt like the longest time. In the distance, I heard Big Ben announce that it was a quarter to nine. But I was almost there.

When I finally arrived in the street where the pub was situated, I could see the glow cast trough the small windows. It beckoned me closer, inviting. In the square of light stood a man, smoking a cigarette. The cherry glowed bright when he inhaled, and tendrils of smoke disappeared into the blackness of the night. My heart leapt when I saw him. The dark hair, the striking face that turned in my direction.

And the broad smile that showed off all his perfectly white teeth.

Chapter 6

Thomas

When Claire arrived she was a vision. I hadn't stopped dreaming about her since I met her, but even though I had traced her features in my dreams and kissed her lips a thousand times in my mind, her beauty in person floored me.

It had happened the first time I had seen her, too. How was it possible that someone could be this beautiful? And it wasn't just her external features, either. Yes, she looked like she was a model, like she couldn't be real. But the person she was on the inside was just as beautiful—the night we had spent together on Saturday had recreated everything I thought about what I wanted in life.

I had told myself that I hadn't come here for a woman, and that I wouldn't get involved with anyone because I was going to war. But then I had met Claire, and everything had changed.

She wore a bright red coat that made her stand out, although I would know her face in any crowd. And she came to me with graceful strides, carrying herself toward me with purpose. She was here for me. And I was here for her.

When she reached me, her cheeks were red, her eyes bright and she wore an expression I did not understand. Her hair was a little tousled, making her perfection seem a little disheveled. And in her imperfection lay nothing but more beauty.

Without a word she wrapped her arms around my neck and buried her face against my shoulder.

"Is everything alright?" I asked, closing my arms around her petite body, feeling her shudder against me.

She didn't say anything, she merely nodded. For some time, she didn't let go. I breathed in, taking in her scent, committing it to memory for those nights in the trenches when hell would breathe its rotten breath in my face. So that I could think back to when my world was perfect.

"It is, now," she finally said.

She was out of breath, as if she had been running the entire distance from wherever she lived to here.

When she finally pulled away from me, I took her hand and pressed my lips to her knuckles. I looked her in the eyes, and a smile spread across her face, making her even more beautiful than she already was. How quickly she had become my sun.

"Shall we go inside?" I asked.

She nodded. "Please."

Tonight, The Bell was a lot quieter than it had been on Saturday. It was during the week and people still tried to maintain a semblance of normalcy. The war had caused a lot of chaos, and the only way to stay sane was to continue with life as much as possible.

Claire and I found a quiet table toward the back of the bar. Tonight, there was no music playing. The pub was filled with the muffled sound of conversation and laughter, combined with the clink of glasses and the occasional opening and shutting of the door.

"Will you get in trouble for this?" I asked Claire when we sat down, each with a cup of coffee in front of us. Neither of us had felt like drinking beer. We weren't here to lose our inhibitions, rather to find ourselves in each other's eyes.

Claire shook her head. "I don't want to talk about that, not now. Just let me enjoy being in your presence for a moment."

I smiled at her and reached for her cheek, touching her delicate skin. It was smooth and flawless, as if made from porcelain. But she was soft and warm to the touch, like a real-life doll.

"Tell me about you, about your life in America, about what you have left behind in order to fight someone else's war."

The way she said it made my heart ache. It was as if she understood part of me that I wasn't sure I understood myself.

"My family owns a ranch in Montana, acre upon acre of rich soil, green rolling hills and a lake nestled between them." I closed my eyes for a moment and I was back home. The sun beat down on my brow, the strong body of a stallion sat between my knees and I could smell the incoming storm on the wind. When I opened my eyes, she was staring at me with a look of wonder on her face and I remembered myself. "We have horses and cows, and a breeding program for both. Horses have always been my passion, and while I understand the cattle business, I have always preferred animals that are more intelligent, and that I can build a connection with."

Claire hung on my every word as I spoke.

"And what of your family? Tell me about them."

"I have two sisters, both younger, and we get on very well. I love them with all my heart. They were terrified when I told them I was coming to the United Kingdom to fight in the war."

"I can imagine," Claire said, in a soft voice. "It's terrifying to think that you are heading out to sacrifice yourself."

I shook my head. "I don't see it that way. We are here to help, and because of the enforced allied armies, victory is imminent."

Claire smiled, but it didn't reach her eyes and I imagined she wasn't quite sure if she could believe me.

"What about you?" I said. "You seem reluctant to speak of your family."

Claire nodded. "It's difficult to speak ill of my father as he is very well respected in our community. But the truth is, we don't see eye to eye and I feel like a prisoner more than a daughter."

I raised my eyebrows. These were harsh words. But her face was serious, and I wondered what she was risking to be here with me tonight.

"When the war is over, I'm going to run," Claire said. She leaned a little closer to me, dropping her voice. Again, her face was so serious, there was no way to conclude anything but that she was telling the truth.

"It's a very dangerous thing to do, and very brave if you manage."

The termination crossed her features. "I will manage it. I have too. There is no way I can allow him to dictate the rest of my life. I'm almost eighteen, and I want to know what it's like to live for myself."

"Where will you go?" I asked. This woman surprised me every time I spoke to her. Not only was she attractive, popular, and clearly a favorite among her peers, but she was also interesting and funny. Intelligent and educated. But that wasn't all. She was also determined and stubborn, and I imagined that someone like Claire would be able to get far in life. If not through the help of others, then through her own doing.

Claire pulled up her shoulders in an elegant shrug. "Anywhere. I don't know yet, I haven't thought of the particulars. I worry that the war will continue for a long time, still. But Ireland is closest. Maybe it's just silly, but I dream of escaping to a place where passion overrides decorum."

It sounded to me like Claire's life had been very strict for a very long time. And I wished that I could impart some of the freedom I had grown up with to her. I wished I could show her what it's had been like to taste the wind, to know that I could ride wherever it blew me.

"To be honest with you, I don't care where I go, as long as I'm far away from here."

Suddenly, an idea dawned on me. Why had it taken me so long to think of this? I took Claire's hands, both of them in mine.

"What about America?" I asked.

Claire looked at me, a frown on her face.

"America? What on earth would a girl like me do in America?"

I squeezed her hands. "Whatever you pleased," I said. "Come home with me. When the war is over, I'll come for you and steal you away. I'll take you to the ranch with me. We can build a new life. We can stand side by side and carve out our own path. We can grow old together, and when the sun sets on our time you can look back and know that you had a life. Let me give you a life, Claire."

Her face was full of wonder and awe as I spoke, her eyes shimmering and her perfectly red lips splitting into a smile.

"You'll come back for me?" she asked.

"I promise."

She leaned forward, threw her arms around my neck, and kissed me. The gesture was so childlike, so wild and free. So sincere. I knew in my heart that this was the right thing. Claire was perfect. Perfectly groomed, perfectly bred, perfectly educated. And for all that was worth, she was perfectly unhappy.

She belonged with me, in a place where she could be free. And I wanted her by my side. I wouldn't part with her for all the money in the world.

"Come with me," Claire said, when she broke the kiss. Her face had changed, her eyes had deepened in color until they seemed almost evergreen and the intensity had grown around us, so that the atmosphere was thick.

I stood, letting her take my hand and lead me away. Fire danced between our fingers, and pulled thin between us like taffy when she moved away from me as we walked.

I didn't know where she was taking me. But I knew where we were going, as two souls who had become one, together. I wasn't sure how this had happened. Or exactly when. Or why now, in the middle of all this death and destruction, I had met the one person that made me feel alive.

All that I knew was that if I didn't have Claire in my life, it wouldn't be a life at all.

Chapter 7

Claire

I wanted to be with Thomas in every sense of the word. He had asked me to go with him to the Americas. And it sounded like a dream come true. I had always been very British, a woman proud of her country.

But if I had to leave my heritage behind for the sake of finding happiness, I would. And to go with Thomas, to live in his life of freedom and adventure, was something I hadn't dared dream about since I had met him.

Now, he wanted to take me home. And I was going to go with him. I would run away, I would leave my father and all his rules behind, and we would run until we couldn't run anymore. Until the sun of Montana kissed my skin, leaving a trail of heat behind for Thomas to follow.

He held my hand as we left The Bell and fire danced on my palm, weaving through his fingers. Did he feel it, too? It was consuming me alive. And I needed to be with him. I needed him to make me his, so that when he left, there would be a part of him that would remain until he came for me again.

I wanted a memory with him that would never fade, a memory I would never have with anyone else.

We walked a few blocks through the city, until we arrived at a small apartment building. I climbed the stairs, Thomas following right behind me.

"Where are we?" Thomas asked.

"It's an apartment my father uses to accommodate his business associates when they travel to London. I stole the key."

I wondered if Thomas thought I had planned for this, now that I had admitted I had taken my father's key. If he thought something terrible of me, he didn't show it when I glanced over my shoulder at him.

The truth was, I had taken the key purely because I had wanted somewhere we could be alone when we were tired of being in public, having to put on masks for everyone that might see us. After all, I was an English girl and he was an American soldier. Not everyone would agree with our friendship.

The Americans were allies but not everyone thought of them as friends.

When I unlocked the door, I walked in and Thomas followed, closing the door behind him.

"I don't want you to think of me as someone who arranged this with a motive in mind," I blurted out. "I am not that sort of girl, and I—"

Thomas quieted me with a kiss. I froze for a moment before I melted against him.

"I could never think badly of you Claire," he said. "Anything but. You are wonderful in my eyes. Lovely in every way."

I smiled at him, relieved.

He looked at me, and his eyes changed. They became deeper, darker, and they were filled something that caused me to shiver. He pushed his hand underneath my hair, his palm searing hot on my skin, and he kissed me again.

And in that kiss, he said everything he hadn't said in words. He felt about me the same way I felt about him. He wanted me, ached for me, just the way I had for him since our first meeting. And he was here with me, just the same way I had meant to be here with him when I pulled him away from the pub.

"Is this too much?" I asked in a whisper when Thomas broke the kiss.

He shook his head and ran his other hand down my arm. How was it possible that a mere touch could give me goosebumps and make me lose my train of thought?

When Thomas looked into my eyes again, the atmosphere grew so thick between us I could barely breathe. I didn't want to breathe.

He kissed me again, and I felt as though I was on fire. My skin was hot, I melted. Warmth flushed through my body and pooled between my legs.

"Thomas pulled me against him, and I felt him. He was erect, as eager for me as I was for him. But I didn't want to be with him because of frustration, or of needing an escape. I wanted to be with him because I needed to be as close to him as humanly possible.

When he unbuttoned my coat, my breath caught. I had never been with a man before, and although I had dreamed about it, and talked about it with my friends, this was new. This was different.

This was terrifying.

"I'll go slowly," Thomas whispered in my ear and a small moan escaped my throat. How was it that he already knew my mind?

I shrugged out of the coat and it fell to the floor. Thomas reached for the button on my blouse and I ran my hands up his sides, feeling the stiff material of his uniform, and his taut body beneath it. The muscles moved under his skin as he lifted his arms and undid my blouse.

When he undressed me, he didn't stare at my body as if it was an object of obsession, as if I was nothing more than something he could covet, own, or demand. I didn't know why I had assumed it would be like that.

When a man had ruled my whole life, treating me as a possession, it was hard to imagine that someone else could treat me as a gift.

"You're beautiful, Claire," Thomas said to me. His voice was thick, his lips parted and he swallowed twice before he kissed me again.

As he kissed me, his hands roamed my body. He ran his fingers along my shoulder, tracing my collarbone, and slowly he moved onto my chest, as if quick movements would scare me away.

Perhaps they would have.

When he slid his hand onto my breast, I gasped. I had never been touched by a man like this before and my skin was on fire. It was as if a furnace raged between us, engulfing everything that I was.

I lifted my hands and tried to concentrate on undoing Thomas's shirt. That was the next step, wasn't it? But it was hard to concentrate with him touching me like that, his hands moving, and my body responding in ways I had never felt before. A blush crept over my entire body, and I stepped from side to side, scissoring my thighs, aware of what was happening between them.

When Thomas's shirt was undone, I pushed it off his shoulders and I had to stop and stare. He was at peak physical condition, everything a soldier of top caliber would be. And he was most definitely the very image of Adonis, carved by the good Lord himself.

Thomas put his finger underneath my chin and lifted my face so that he could look into my eyes. I blushed, knowing I had stared at him like a fool.

But he said nothing of my foolishness. In his eyes was only adoration and he kissed me again before he took my hand and led me through the apartment to the small bedroom that was adjacent to the front room. He gently nudged me down so that I sat on the bed, then sat down beside me. He kissed me, and together we somehow lay back.

His hands slid down my body and I lost my breath when he slid his hands over my hip bone and onto my leg. He pulled up my skirt until my undergarments showed. I blushed, but he continued, his eyes burrowing into mine. My breathing was shallow and erratic. Slowly he pushed his hand up toward the apex of my thighs.

When he cupped my sex, a moan escaped my mouth and I curled against him, my body moving of its own volition.

"Is this okay?" he asked softly.

I nodded. It was more than okay.

Thomas was patient with me. He moved slowly, he was careful when he touched me, and when he went about undressing me, he made me feel like he was unwrapping a present, taking his time, making me ache for his touch.

I took off my own bra.

Thomas smiled at me, and kicked off his pants. And I stared at him, shocked. I had spoken about the male body to my friends, but I had never seen it, and this was more than I had ever thought I could want. I blushed and averted my eyes.

But Thomas still didn't think any of this was silly, and I was relieved that he ignored how much of a child I was being. He crawled over me, the mattress dipping beneath us. His body hovered over me, and he positioned himself at my entrance.

I held my breath.

"It's going to hurt for a little bit," he said.

Fear gripped me for a moment. But when he slid in, the pinch was overridden by the pleasure and I cried out.

Thomas froze, looking at me in terror.

"No, don't stop," I gasped.

And he did as I asked. He started moving inside of me, and I felt full. When I opened my eyes, his focus was on my face and he looked worried. I reached up, cupping his cheeks, and pulled him down to kiss me. His chest was against my breasts, nothing between us, and I had never felt closer and more connected to someone ever in my life.

As he kissed me, he moved inside of me, pushing me to the edge of the unknown. And when I thought I couldn't go any further, he took me in his hands and I fell. Knowing that he would catch me.

The night was long, and we were huddled together, cocooned by the darkness. We were pressed against each other, so close that I had no idea who I had been before Thomas, and unsure of who I would be without him when he left. But I wouldn't think about that, now.

I would think of who he was to me, and what we would be once the war was over. I focused on how his body felt against mine, his muscles so hard, but his touch so gentle. I focused on how we had come together, merging until we were one glorious being and so close, it was unclear where I stopped, and he began.

When it was all over, when Thomas had lost himself in the raptures of pleasure and he had led me to the depth of our sex and back again another time, we lay together, wrapped in the blankets on the bed. I lay with my head on his chest, his heart beating against my cheek, and his arm wrapped around my shoulders, holding me close.

"Tell me about the ranch again," I said softly into the darkness. "Tell me how beautiful it is."

"When the sun comes up in the morning, it touches the fields with a golden finger. The grass that seemingly lost its color during the night, regains life and the green explodes in a celebration of color, welcoming the dawn. When there is dew, the hills wear it like jewelry, inviting the sun back after the long night."

"I love the way you speak of home," I said. "You make it sound like it's the best place in the world."

"I used to think it was the most beautiful thing I had ever seen," Thomas said, his eyes closed, his fingers playing on the skin of my arm.

"Used to?" I asked.

"That was before I met you," he said, opening his eyes. He looked at me and his eyes were pools of black that I lost myself in. He kissed me and I let him taste me, explore my mouth, and he kissed me again as if for the first time. Whenever he touched me, he touched me with the same awe as if he had never experienced me before.

"I'll wait for you, Thomas," I said, when he finally broke the kiss. "However long it takes for you to get back. I'll wait."

"A man has never had something as worthy to fight for, Claire," he said, and my heart leaped. "I will find you. And I will make you mine."

Chapter 8

Amelia

On Wednesday morning I unlocked the shop and walked in, closing the door behind me again. Usually, Arthur was here since the crack of dawn, digging in some box he'd unearthed with new antiques we could label and sell. He would always be so caught up in his explorations that he would be surprised to see me.

But since he was away this week, the shop was dark. I switched on the lights and smiled as the light bounced off the antique objects. I walked to the vintage cash register and put away my handbag.

The morning routine was my favorite, waking up the store after a long night of sleep. I opened the door and pulled vintage chairs outside, placing a delicate china cup and a matching teapot on a small side table and an old book on the chair.

On the other side, I set out a chalk board with my little quote of the day. Objects disintegrate, but memories last forever.

I put the chalk down and dusted my hand.

"Morning, Amelia!" Mrs. Lopez called from across the road and I waved at her. She passed the shop on her way to the bakery every morning. Sometimes, she brought me a doughnut or a scone.

Inside, I opened the old school cash register, counted the float and made sure we were ready to do business. It was amazing how many people bought from an antique shop. I had always loved antiques and had shopped for them often, but I had thought I was one of the few.

Still, Arthur and his nostalgia shop here in the smallest town I had ever been in, did swimmingly well.

MY SWEETHEART

I walked to the stereo and switched it on so that music could fill the shop. It brought everything to life. I decided on Pink Martini, bringing the taste of Europe into the shop as the French words danced from the speakers, twirling and skipping between the antique furniture and objects.

Walking between the displays, I admired every item—dusting, admiring, and adjusting every item.

I loved working here. There was something about the past that tickled my fancy. I loved the idea of people living lives in times gone by, how they had gone about their business, what they had loved or loathed, and the traces left behind for us to find and follow in this modern era. I wasn't interested in technology or the fast pace of my world. I preferred to slow down and look at how far we'd come, and what we had endured that had brought us here.

The store phone rang and I hurried to answer it.

"I thought you'd be in by now," Arthur said. "How are things?"

"Great," I said. "Everything is just how it should be."

"You're a star. And my online order?"

"It arrived yesterday. Along with a box of trinkets someone dropped off. I'm going to log it in today and put it out for us."

"I'll be back on the weekend so you can show me what you've found."

I agreed and we ended the conversation. When I was done talking to Arthur, I walked to the door and turned the sign from 'Closed' to 'Open.'

I fetched the box from the back room. Someone had brought it in yesterday, telling me they'd found it in their garage and weren't going to go through the trouble of getting rid of it in a yard sale. I was always happy to get boxes like this. Often, it contained junk. But sometimes, you found gems.

And that was what I was hoping for today.

I cut the tape with a knife and opened the flaps, peering into the box.

Immediately, I knew this was a good find. It was filled with gadgets that looked like it might have belonged to a dentist. I unpacked it, checking for rust and taking photos. I would have to research some of these and see what they were and how to price them.

A few figurines appeared next, in good condition and they were easy enough to put a price on.

There was a stack of books. No first editions, but I hadn't expected there to be. Some of them were in French, one in German. And there were classics like Moby Dick and Robinson Crusoe, all with their material covers, bound with string as they had done it in the old days, before the modern presses came with their hot glue and mass production prints.

At the bottom of the box, I found an envelope. The paper was thick, yellowed with time. I pressed it to my nose and breathed in. I loved the smell of old paper. There was something floral about it, too. As if the sender had spritzed it with perfume.

When I turned it over, the seal was still intact. It was a wax seal, stamped with what seemed to be a family crest. A falcon with wings spread, and smaller symbols I couldn't make out. I ran my fingers over the seal. It was very rare to still find unbroken seals. They were usually all opened.

On the front, a name was written in ink, the letters dramatic, slanted, and elegant. I imagined elegant hands writing this with a quill, sealing the envelope so the contents remained unseen by eyes other than that of her lover.

Curiosity tugged at me. I wanted so badly to open the envelope, to see what the letter said. Suppose it was a title deed? Or a letter naming someone as an heir to an incredible fortune? Or perhaps it was a business letter.

Or a love letter.

MY SWEETHEART

I slid my fingers over the seal again. I wanted to know what this letter said.

But with the seal still intact, Arthur would love to open it himself. Maybe it would be best for him to open it when he came back. He would be here on the weekend, it wasn't so far away.

Although, it was far too long for me to have to wait to find out what the letter was about.

For a moment, I considered opening it. But then I put it down on the counter. This was for Arthur to open. It was his shop.

The bell above the door rang with the first customer of the day and I smiled. I looked up to see Beth coming toward the counter, two Styrofoam cups in her hands. Her brown hair was piled on her head in a messy bun and she already wore the Cuppa apron that the barista's wore at the shop next door.

"I come bearing gifts," she said.

"You're a star," I said, walking around the counter and hugging her before taking the cup. When I sipped it, I smiled.

"Chai latte."

"Just the way you nerds like it," Beth said, and sipped her own cup. She looked around. "I don't know how you survive in here. It's so dark."

"It's intimate," I said.

"Yeah—well, no. It's dark. I love that you love what you do, though. But better you than me, my friend." She hopped up onto the counter, a move I had stopped fighting her on it weeks ago.

"So, what's new?" Beth asked.

"If there was anything new, you would have heard it through the grapevine," I said. "You can't keep secrets in this town."

"Maybe I'm here to start the gossip," Beth said. "If you can't beat 'em, join 'em."

I laughed. "Either way, I have nothing to report. Except that a stern looking guy came in on Monday and demanded to know how I was."

"Handsome, graying, looks like he'll chastise you for just existing if you don't do it right?"

"Yeah," I said with a grin.

"That's Craig Owen. He's an ass. He gives me hell, too. He was in here again the other day, probably just after he left you. He was friends with Arthur's son and he stuck around even though no one wants him."

"Everyone has someone that wants them," I said.

"Poetic of you," Beth said and drank more of her coffee. "But not this guy. Does he look like best friend material?"

Before I could answer, Beth noticed the letter and picked it up. "What's this?"

"I found it in the box I unpacked this morning."

"So, it's old."

"Everything in here is old, Beth," I said with a laugh.

Beth turned the letter over in her hands. "And it's sealed."

I nodded and walked to her, hopping onto the counter, too. Arthur would kill me if he saw me doing this.

"So, open it," Beth said. "Are you dying to know what it says?"

"I am," I said, nodding. "But I'll leave it to Arthur. He's crazy about these things."

Beth studied the handwriting. "It has to be from a woman. No man I know writes like that."

"But men were different back then."

"Back when?" Beth asked.

I shrugged. "I don't actually know. It could be anywhere in the last century, to be honest. Maybe even older."

Beth picked up her coffee and sipped it again. My tea was getting cold but I had forgotten about it.

"Is it worth a lot if it stays sealed?"

I shook my head. "They'll have to open it, anyway, to know."

"So, open it then," Beth said. "I don't even care about this stuff and I'm curious now."

I laughed. I wanted to open it so badly.

"And you know Arthur will just ruin it."

I looked at Beth. I had mentioned to her before how clumsy Arthur could be. What if he ripped the paper when he opened the seal? Or worked with dirty hands, or something? I knew I was looking for excuses just to convince myself, but it was working. I knew I could do a good job of opening it.

I had finesse.

"Okay, okay, I'll open it," I said.

Beth clapped her hands like a child, excited. I hopped off the counter and walked to the back room to find a knife with a thin blade so I could carefully pry open the seal. I returned and Beth and I hunched together over the counter as I carefully slid the knife underneath the wax.

I worked slowly, loosening it bit by bit. I held my breath and noticed that Beth was as engrossed as I was.

Finally, it was open, and to my credit, the paper wasn't damaged at all. I patted myself on the back and opened the flap.

"And?" Beth asked.

"Give me a chance to take it out," I laughed, as I pulled out the letter.

It was written on equally thick, creamy paper, that had been folded across the width twice before over once. I took it out carefully and opened it.

"This is crazy," Beth said. "I always thought this shit was so boring, but I'm all over it right now. Is this why you do it?"

I nodded. "We don't always find things like this. But it's pretty cool when we do, huh?"

"It's awesome," Beth said.

I tried not to get my hopes up that this letter was something worthwhile. It could be nothing, just scribbles on a page, like a diary entry or a letter to ask for a visit. But the seal and the elegant handwriting made it seem so formal.

And I wished that it was something prolific, something that would excite me. A secret of days gone by that was only to be unraveled, now.

When I opened the paper, carefully unfolding it, the same dramatically, curved handwriting filled the paper.

"What is it?" Beth asked, craning her neck to see. I turned so that she could see the contents as well.

"A letter," I said. "To a man."

"Oh, my goodness," Beth said. "How can you even read that writing? What does it say?"

I had no trouble making out the words, so I cleared my throat and started to read, "My Sweetheart, my dear Thomas."

Chapter 9

Claire
Four months later

'*My Sweetheart,*
My dear Thomas,

You appeared in my dreams again last night. Sometimes, when I close my eyes, yours is the only face I see. It drives me mad with longing, knowing that we will be separated for so long, without any knowledge of what our future might hold.

But this dream was different than the others. There was no terror and no pain, no blood and no war. We were on your porch in Montana, hand in and as the sun sank behind the horizon. There wasn't a care in the world, the terrors of reality so far removed. We were side by side and that was all that mattered. We looked out over your ranch to your fields that were painted pink by the setting sun.

I was at ease. We were together. You were holding my hand and you were real.

We had children, too, in my dream. Children that grew up knowing only peace and prosperity. They were in their beds, sleeping soundly, because every night they could put their heads on their pillows without worrying that tomorrow may never come.

It was a glorious dream.

But when I woke I remembered you were gone, and I was alone, the fear soon creeping back again. I try not to let it cripple me. I try to be strong. But as the time drags on and you're not back yet, I start to fear that our dreams of a life together may never come true. I know you will want me to be strong. But some days I truly do not know how.

Where are you? Are you safe? Do you think of me as often as I think of you? There are some nights where I fear that our time together was so fleeting, that your memory of me will be fleeting as well. But I know in my heart that your love me for is as unfaltering as mine.

I pray for you before I close my eyes at night. And when I open them in the morning. And I hope and plead with God to keep you safe on the battlefield. I care more about your safety than I do about liberation from the Germans. I know that I am wrong to feel that way, but you have become everything to me in a very short time. You have changed my life forever. You made me a promise I have not and cannot forget.

It has been four months and three days since I've seen you. I can't help but count every hour as it passes without delivering you back to me. I don't know how much longer I have to wait, but I know I will wait forever if that is what it takes to see you again. To kiss your lips. To feel your arms around me. My heart beats only for you.

I am safe. And wherever you are, I hope you are as well.
Love Always,
Your English Girl,
Claire Whiteside.

I put my pen down and sighed, leaning back in my chair. I closed my eyes and pictured Thomas's face. It had been so long since I'd seen him. The memories I had of him were frayed at the edges, I visited them so often. Sometimes, when I thought about the night we had spent together, I didn't feel the exhilaration as strongly as I used to.

And it terrified me to think that my memories with him were slipping through my fingers. Or that he would return as someone other than the man that had said goodbye to me the very next morning.

But I couldn't think so negatively. I had to hold fast to the promise that he had made me, that he would come back for me and take me home, making me his wife.

I opened my eyes again and folded the letter carefully, tucking it into an envelope. Carefully, I wrote the address Thomas had given me, making sure not to make an error, and I turned the envelope around. With a candle and matchstick, I dripped melted wax on the envelope, sealing it shut.

The family stamp was on my desk, a heavy piece of metal with an ivory inset, and it had our crest on it. The Falcon, the chain and the scroll. I pressed it into the wax, leaving an indentation behind that would tell the world which family the letter had come from. I hoped that our family name, my father's connections, would carry the letter further than any other letter would be able to travel.

"Are you getting my letters, Thomas?" I asked softly, holding the envelope in both hands. "Are you still alive?"

It had been a long time since I had heard from him. And every passing day I didn't receive any answers to my letters, I had to stop myself from fearing the worst.

I stood up from my desk and walked to my closet. Shrugging into a coat, I buttoned it up, then wrapped a scarf around my neck and put a hat on my head. It had since turned to winter, the frost and snow dampening spirits as the war raged on. And I hated the idea of braving the cold.

But I had to send this letter off. I had to give Thomas the reassurance that I was still here, waiting for him. That I would always be here. If he was coming home, he would come home to a woman that loved him.

It was well after lunch time and my mother had locked herself away in her parlor. She spent much time alone lately and I wondered if it was to contemplate the horrors of war and pray for the soldiers, as she had so often told my father, or if it was to escape the man himself.

My father had become worse in the last few months, clamping down on the household, and he wore a permanent scowl on his face.

He had been right when he told me, so many months ago, that war changed even the best of men.

I wondered if he knew that it was changing him, too.

I walked to the front door, careful not to be spotted. The servants were cleaning the rooms and preparing supper. My father was in his office, going over paperwork that had been sent to him from the North, and the front of the house was quiet. I opened the door and slipped out.

When I had first started sneaking out, I had been bitter about my father treating me like a prisoner. There had been damage after the bombings, yes, and everything had changed since the soldiers had arrived. But it hadn't been nearly as bad, then.

Now, my father's fears were more justified. But I had to mail the letter.

I walked through the streets. They were all but abandoned. The face of the city had changed in the past few months. Half of London was boarded up, with windows broken, doors locked. Even the buildings themselves seemed dragged down by sorrow. With the winter here, there was barely any sun, but some days I felt as though the sun refused to show its face, turning away from the horrors of war.

A group of men stood in the street, arguing loudly about something. Once upon a time, I would have walked past them with my head held high, knowing they would pay attention to me, knowing that I was a woman to be desired. Now, I didn't want to be desired by anyone. No one other than Thomas.

And the men looked for ways to distract themselves. With the pain and suffering around us, it seemed as though it stripped the nation of their humanity and they had started doing things they would never have considered before the war.

I gave the men a wide berth, ducking into an alleyway to get to the mailbox I needed to reach.

Finally, I made it, and dropped the letter into the red mailbox. I watched it slip into the darkness and silently prayed that it would reach Thomas, that he would be safe and sound when it did. And that he would come back to me.

On the way back home, it started snowing. White flakes swirled down from a grim sky and the temperature dropped. The world was soon transformed by the flurry and I shivered in my coat, huddling it tighter around me. It took me longer to get home, with the wind seemingly blowing right through me.

When I finally got home, closing the door quietly behind me, my father waited in the entrance hall. One hand held a pipe and the other was tucked into his pocket.

My stomach dropped. I had hoped he wouldn't notice my absence.
"Where were you?" he demanded.
"I went for tea," I lied weakly. "With Dorothy."
That wasn't the truth at all. Dorothy and her family had left town a few weeks ago, going to the country where it might be safer from potential bombing. But Dorothy wasn't in the same circle as Ruth and I, and my father didn't care for Dorothy's parents. And I hadn't mentioned their plan to him, or that I was starting to lose people I cared about.

"You left without asking permission?"

I had no fight left in me. To stand up against my father would only turn into another argument and as the time had dragged on, the city had come undone at the seams and I hadn't heard anything from Thomas. I didn't have the energy.

"I didn't want to disturb you. And mother was praying."

My father narrowed his eyes at me.

"How many times do I have to tell you, Claire? You can't go out there alone. It's no place for a young lady. If something happened to you, I would never recover."

I frowned. I wanted to ask what he meant, if he meant emotionally, or if it would put his reputation at stake.

But I wouldn't ask the question if I wasn't ready for the answer. Besides, he was my father. Despite his need for social acknowledgement, I believed that he did care for me in his own way. And I wouldn't pressure him to verbalize it.

"I am going to spend some time in my room, if I'm allowed," I said.

My father nodded. Since I wasn't arguing with him, he had nothing more to add to the conversation. An argument could not be one-sided.

He nodded once and I walked past him toward my bedroom. I felt as though I was thawing now that I was in the warm house again, and I closed myself in my room. I leaned against the door, and closed my eyes for a moment. I had to remain strong, and be the headstrong girl Thomas had met. I couldn't give in to anything. No matter how difficult the times became.

I had known it would be difficult to have someone in battle while I waited at home, hoping every day that he wouldn't leave me for good. If he died, I wouldn't even receive a telegram, it would be sent home to his family and I would never know.

So, I would believe that he was still alive and well, and that he would come for me, just as he had promised.

Thomas was a man of his word, and I was a woman of mine. And this war would not last forever. It would eventually end, and when it did, we would live happily ever after.

Just like the couples did in the romance books I read. I had to hold onto the fantasy, because I was worried that if I looked at reality, I would lose all hope. Then surely, all would be lost.

Chapter 10

Thomas

I had known that war would be hard. We were killing other, pointing a gun and shooting because they wore different colors, because they had different beliefs. This wasn't my first rodeo, after all. I had enlisted a while ago and we had been on a battle front before.

But this was something else. This was hell on earth. I hadn't expected to come here and have the horrors haunt me every time I closed my eyes. I hadn't expected to see the faces of those I had killed, to feel as though I had somehow betrayed them.

I hadn't expected the crimson color of blood to tinge every waking thought I had, and every dream once I fell asleep.

The more time I spent in Europe, marching through muddy fields, hiding out in abandoned houses or running at the enemy in small towns, the more I lost perspective. Every day was a fight for survival, and I had to remember what I was doing it all for. I wasn't here to fight for another country, to help the United Kingdom. Now, I was here to fight my way back to the girl that had stolen my heart without even trying. I had never intended to have my heart stolen, but no one planned for these things. If I had planned, I would have ensured that I had met Claire somewhere safe, somewhere we could be together.

Somewhere far away from this hell that surrounded us and the war that forced us apart.

Sometimes, I had no idea how long it had been since I had seen her face. The days and weeks blurred into each other, becoming one long movie of horror as we continued to trudge through the countryside and fight whoever we could find. Sometimes we didn't sleep for days on end.

Sometimes I was so tired, I thought that if I lay down right on the spot and slept, I wouldn't even care if someone came and speared me.

But then, when we found a place to rest, found a couple of rations that we could share, and I could think clearly again, I knew that it had only been a handful of months. Four, if I had counted correctly.

For long months away from the place that I now called home.

But I hadn't heard from Claire. Not once, not a single letter. Not since the first couple of weeks since I had been gone. And if I had to be honest about it, it terrified me. What if she had forgotten about me? What if she had moved on? Our romance had been so quick, coming into being out of nothing, it seemed. And we had only seen each other twice. Even though we had felt everything for each other while we were in each other's arms, even though I had seen myself spending the rest of my life with her, I was terrified that the small amount of time we had been able to spend together just hadn't been enough to keep me in the forefront of her mind.

What if she had decided she didn't want this? After the war was over and I was allowed to go back home, I would go to London to try to find her.

But one of my biggest nightmares was that she wouldn't be there when I did. That she would have moved on, or worse, that she would have found someone else.

War was everywhere and it was terrible all over. And there was a chance that Claire would not survive. But the idea of her dying seemed surreal. It didn't scare me nearly as much as it should have. Rather, it was the idea of her forgetting about me that terrified me.

After we had walked for days on end, we finally found an abandoned barn. The farmhouse had been burned down by enemy troops, but the barn was still intact. The animals were gone, and the bar and smelled of stale hay. But since we had come to war, my standards of comfort had changed completely.

The barn was dry, there was a roof over our heads, and after a couple of Scouts had surrounded the area, they came back with word that it was safe. For the first time in a while, we could breathe.

One of the soldiers handed out rations, a small piece of bread, and bits of dried meat. We hadn't had a proper meal in a long time, but this tasted like heaven when I took a bite.

"Oh, my goodness, I don't think I've ever tasted something as great as this," Harry said, sitting next to me. We were in a corner of the barn, our backsides on some hay, and our backs against the wooden barn wall.

"I know," I said. This food was like a feast to us.

"Do you think we are going to have to walk far after this?" Harry asked.

I shook my head. "I think we can rest here for a while. We need to regain our strength."

Harry nodded.

We sat in silence for a while. My mind drifted to Claire again and I felt a pang in my chest. Where was she now? Was she thinking about me?

"You're very quiet these days," Harry said.

I pulled up my shoulders. "It's difficult to keep your spirits up when there is war raging all around us. I guess Dave has a way of tainting everything black.

"It's not about the war though, is it?" Harry knew me better than that. We had only met when we had arrived in England. He had come from Texas. But as the time continued here on foreign soil, where we fought just to stay alive, Harry and I had become quite close.

"It's that girl isn't it," Harry asked, when I didn't answer. "The one from the bar?"

I nodded. "Claire."

"I have to say, she really is something. But I didn't think you would be so serious about her so quickly. And a British girl, too."

I pulled up my shoulders. "There is something about her. I don't know how to explain it, but I know when I look at her that I want her for the rest of my life."

Harry nodded. "Love can do that to you. Does she feel the same way?"

I sighed. "I thought so, yes. But now, I'm not so sure. I haven't heard from her in a while."

"How long has it been?" Harry asked.

I sighed. "Months." I fished for a photo of Claire and pulled it out. She had given it to me when she had said goodbye that morning, telling me that she didn't want me to ever forget her face, that she wanted me to burn it into my mind. As if I could ever forget her. When I closed my eyes, I could still feel her skin under my fingertips, still smell her floral scent from the perfume she wore. I could hear her laughter in my ears.

"Can I see?" Harry asked, yanking me out of my thoughts.

I nodded and handed him the photo. Harry had seen her before, of course. But now, he whistled through his teeth.

"She really is something. Pretty as a picture. I don't blame you for falling for her."

I nodded again, not sure what to say. The truth was, I had no idea what had happened. Claire had written me so often at first, the letters coming frequently. And they had kept me going, given me hope. Those first few weeks had been awful, with death everywhere and I had felt like I had been yanked away from a fairytale world and dropped into a harsh reality. Her letters had saved me time and time again.

And they had smelled like her, as if she had spritzed her perfume on them. I had traced her handwriting with my thumb so many nights, I was sure I could imitate it in my sleep. And when I touched her writing like that, following her elegant scrawl, it was like I was back with her again, tracing her curves with my hands.

Damn, I missed her dearly. When I thought about her, I thought about taking her back to the ranch. Growing old with her. I thought about the sun on our faces, and not a care in the world.

"I'm sorry to hear it," Harry said.

"Hear what?" I asked. I had thought about Claire and I hadn't kept track of the conversation.

"That you haven't heard from her. These kinds of things happen all the time."

I frowned. "What things?" I asked, even though I knew what Harry was going to say. And I was irritated. What did he know?

"How long can you expect a girl to wait? Especially at a time like this. I've heard so many stories where soldiers go to war and when they come home, their woman just isn't there."

I shook my head, trying to swallow my anger. It wasn't fair of me to get angry with Harry, he was just telling me what happened. And it was realistic, too. But I was tired and scared and hungry and wasn't in the mood to look at reality. I wanted to dream about Claire, to imagine that she was still waiting for me back in London.

"You don't know her," I said, and even I was impressed with how controlled my voice was. "She's not like that. She won't do that to me."

"You've only known her a couple of months, and you've barely seen her enough times for you to know who she is."

I took the photo back from Harry, whether he was done looking at it or not, and tucked it into my pocket. I tried to fight the anxiety that clawed at my chest. Claire wasn't going to abandon me. She wasn't going to move on and find something better. Because there wasn't something better out there, and I knew what I could offer her. And I knew what I felt for her.

And I knew that she had felt it too, she must have. She would not have agreed to me coming back for her if she hadn't.

But I was starting to doubt. The further we went along, the more time passed without me hearing from her, the more I became terrified that this was it. This was my reality now, one in which Claire just didn't exist.

But no, I was going to ignore it. I wasn't going to listen to Harry or allow him to make me doubt. I was already struggling so much. Not knowing what was going on with Claire, or what we were to each other anymore, was so much worse than this war.

It sounded insane to say something like that. After all, Claire was a woman I had barely known before we came to war. Losing her should not have terrified me so much. Feeling so strongly about her should not have happened so soon. But it happened sometimes, where you meet someone who was always meant to be with you, and it didn't matter how much time passed. It was right, from the start.

That was how I felt about Claire. In no time at all, she had become my whole world. And I knew that if I went back to London and found out that she had left me, my whole world would shatter.

I turned away from Harry, trying to lie down get a little sleep. We hadn't slept in almost two days, and I was exhausted. I told myself that was probably half the reason I was so scared. Yeah, I hadn't heard from her, but letters hardly found us here on the battlefield when no one knew exactly where we were. And maybe she'd had to flee, maybe she wasn't able to write letters. But she had not forgotten about me.

Yes, I would hold onto these excuses rather than to accept that Claire had forgotten me.

Chapter 11

Amelia

I couldn't forget about the love letter. It was supposed to just be another antique, and something we could put up for sale. But there was something about the words, something about the way they had been written that tugged at my heart. I couldn't imagine feeling that way about someone. Or having someone feel that way about me.

My whole life had been rushed, with nothing but office parties and deadlines. Dating had been thought of as a sideline thing. But even when I had been involved with people, the men had all seemed distracted, as if I was an afterthought.

In this letter, the woman clearly felt so attached to whoever she was writing to, she couldn't imagine a life without him. I had never been able to imagine my life with someone else, let alone without them. I had always been on my own.

And because there was something about this, something that seemed so desperate and so forlorn, I wanted to know more. The letter dated from nineteen forty-two, which meant that the writer could still be alive. And I needed to know more. I simple had to.

Who was she? Did they find each other? How did their life start? And how did it end? I couldn't imagine love in a time of war, where the future was uncertain in so many ways. And I couldn't imagine love that burned so deeply it could transcend anything else.

For two days, the letter haunted me. I had put it in the storage room along with all the other items that needed to be labeled and shelved. I had work to do, I had a shop to run and I had items to log.

But my mind kept wandering back to Claire Whiteside, the woman who had written the letter. And her heart, which may or may not have been broken.

Beth came into the shop on Friday morning, bringing me another Chai Latte.

"How are things going today?" she asked. "Are you glad Arthur is coming back soon, or did you like being alone all week?"

I pulled up my shoulders. "He is quirky to be around and I learned a lot from him. But I enjoyed being able to run the shop on my own this week. Hopefully he'll go back on another expedition soon, and I'll get another chance."

"Imagine, if you get to run your own shop one day," Beth said.

I nodded. Having my own nostalgia shop sounded like a dream come true. But right now, I was glad that Arthur was returning. I wanted to take the time to find out more about the letter and I needed him to man the store while I did that. As it was, I was already spending far too much time with my nose in books, learning about the Second World War. It was something I had always been interested in, but now I looked at the history books through new eyes, trying to imagine what it had to be like to be a woman living in those times, trying to find love.

"You're distracted," Beth pointed out.

I nodded. "It's that letter. It's got my mind in a knot. I want to find out what really happened to them. Do you think they ended up together?"

They thought about it for a moment. "I don't know. It would be great to imagine they did. But it was during the war, wasn't it? I don't know how realistic it is that they found each other again, the statistics are weird."

"Do you know what the statistics are?"

Beth laughed. "No, I'm not a walking history book. I guess I'll have to Google that one. Or go look at the library, I'm sure they'll have more answers than I do."

Until now, I hadn't touched Google, and I hadn't even thought about the library. I had been telling myself that this wasn't anything that I should worry about, that I should move on with my life. It was just an old letter, after all.

But now that they had suggested it, I couldn't help myself. I had to get onto Google and find out what I could.

"I wouldn't even know where to start," I said. "The letter doesn't contain much information when it comes to location. I don't know where she was writing from, or where this person was stationed."

Beth pulled up her shoulders. "See what you can find on Google, and then let it go if you don't find anything. I'm sure that there are hundreds of letters like that, lost all over the world after the war."

I nodded. Beth was probably right. But it was clear that she didn't share the same passion for history as I did. She knew a lot about Pinewood and I had picked her brain for information when I had arrived here. But the only reason she knew so much about the place was because she had grown up here, as had her parents and grandparents and their parents before that. It was a part of her history, her heritage.

"Well, I'm going to head back to the shop and leave you to do your own digging," Beth said.

Usually, I asked her to stay a little longer so that we could chat, gossip about the customers, or laugh about something Arthur said or did. But this time, I was fine having her out of my shop. There weren't any customers, and that would give me time to jump onto the Internet.

As soon as Beth was gone, I opened Google and typed in Claire Whiteside. Of course, a list of names popped up, and there were thousands of them throughout the US. That wasn't going to help me at all. Whether she was living or deceased, I wouldn't know where to start with a list this long.

I thought about it for a moment, and then a thought dawned on me. The letter had been dropped off here, in Pinetown. It didn't matter where it had been written, where it should have been sent to. What mattered was where it had arrived. Even if the letter had been written somewhere else, the fact that it was here meant it had come with someone.

Maybe Pinetown was something I should search.

I searched for Claire Whiteside in Pinetown. But the search brought up nothing. Of course, if she had married the man to whom this letter was addressed, or if she had married anyone else, for that matter, her name would not have been Whiteside anymore.

That would make the search a little more difficult, and I couldn't just type Claire into the Google search bar.

But Pinetown was a small place, and I was pretty sure that if there was any kind of registry, it would be at the old library. Which was exactly what Beth had suggested. I knew that Beth wasn't as interested in this story, particularly, but she was helping me out without knowing it.

I ached to go to the library right away, but I had to stay in the shop and tend to customers. I couldn't just close the shop and do whatever I wanted. No matter how curious I was.

So, I waited until lunchtime. And the worst was that until then, not a single customer came into the store. I would have been able to lock up and go, but I hadn't known that at the beginning of the day, and I didn't want to close our shop and lose business for Arthur just because I was following my own whims.

But at the moment it was lunchtime, I flipped the little sign in the shop door, announcing that it was closed. Locking up, I walked the three blocks to the local library. One thing I loved about Pinetown was how small it was—everything was within walking distance.

"Hello Mrs. Mills," I said with a smile.

"Oh, Amelia!" she said, and I loved the way she said my name. "What a pleasant surprise. What can I help you with?"

"I was wondering if you have anything like a census here, with names of people who used to live here, with marriages, deaths, that sort of thing."

"If you want a census you're going to have to ask favors at City Hall," Mrs. Mills said, thinking. My stomach sank. I wasn't going to get any answers from City Hall, they weren't all about history and research. They were tightlipped and painful. I'd asked a while ago about buildings plans for my apartment and they had such a fit about it that I'd ended up just leaving.

"But if you want something like marriages and deaths, we do have newspaper articles dating back to the eighteen hundreds."

I perked up at that. Maybe that was something I could use. It lessened my chances of really finding someone, but it was way better than nothing.

"And I don't know if you remember Ronny, the kid who worked here for the summer?"

I shook my head. "It must have been before my time."

"Right, well, he was quite a whiz with these things and he installed some kind of fancy system that makes it easier to go through the articles than having to page them by hand. I spent all summer scanning in the articles. Come, I'll show you."

My heart beat in my throat. It was such a long shot. There was more chance that I wouldn't be able to find anything, than that I could find Claire Whiteside at all, or the man she married.

I followed Mrs. Mills through the library and into a small little back room. It had no windows, and in the middle was a large computer with a projector that pointed at a white wall. Mrs. Mill showed me how to access files on the computer, and how it brought up the article and showed it on the wall.

"This is really cool," I said.

Mrs. Mills nodded. "If I'm honest with you, I preferred the old newspapers. It was like holding pieces of the past in your hands, and smelling the memories between the old pages when you touched them. But time moves on, doesn't it?"

I nodded and smiled politely, waiting for Mrs. Mills to leave before I started my search. I went through everything I could think of, from marriages and deaths to new arrivals and advertisements and tragedies.

But there was no Claire Whiteside to be found. And before long, my lunch hour was over.

"Did you find anything?" Mrs. Mills asked, when I walked back toward the front of the library.

"Unfortunately not," I said. My heart was heavy. I had hit a dead-end, there was nothing else for me to find, nothing else to go by.

"Oh, that's a pity, dear. I'm sorry." The phone rang and she excused herself. I listened to her conversation, absently thinking about Claire Whiteside.

"Oh, no. This is the wrong number. You're looking for the Whiteside Guild. Hang on a minute, I'll give you the number."

My ears perked up when I heard Whiteside, and I frowned. I waited until Mrs. Mill gave the caller a phone number and ended the call.

"What's the Whiteside Guild?" I asked.

"Oh, it's a Rose Exhibition held every year where the best gardeners from all over the county come together and show off their roses. It's run by Mrs. Claire Peters."

"Nee Whiteside?" I asked.

Mrs. Mills nodded. "Yes, I believe so. Although I'm not sure, she was Mrs. Peters by the time she arrived in town. I believe she named the Guild after her late mother, or something of the sort."

Mrs. Mills went on about the roses and how well the Guild was doing, but my ears were ringing. Claire Peters? Claire. And she lived in Pinetown?

"I'm sorry, did you say that Claire Peters lives here?"

Mrs. Mills nodded. "She's on the estate just outside of town. You must have seen it, it's got the best garden in the county, with roses that will make anyone swoon."

I hadn't seen the estate, I barely left town and when I had come in, it had been late at night. But I was willing to bet that this was the woman I was looking for. Or at least, I was hoping so. I had to hold onto this last shred of hope, and I wished that it would turn into some kind of lead. Otherwise I would have nothing.

When I left the library, I called Beth.

"Guess what?" I asked.

"You need another latte?"

I rolled my eyes at her stupid comment. "I found her."

"Who?"

"Claire Whiteside! Or at least, I think that's who she is. Was. She's a Peters now."

"Oh, the rose lady."

I ignored that Beth knew this. She wouldn't have known to tell me, anyway. It had been pure coincidence that I had come across this information.

"I'm going to go see her. I want to talk to her, to find out if she's the one who wrote the letter. Are you coming with me?"

Beth laughed. "You're on your own with this one. I love a good intrigue, but I'm not really down for snooping around an old lady's house."

I laughed. "I'm not going to snoop around, just chat to her. But suit yourself. I'll tell you everything whether you want to hear or not, anyway."

Beth laughed. "Looking forward to it."

Chapter 12

Claire

When I opened my eyes, the world was gray. The light that fell through my curtains was tainted with sorrow and it felt like something heavy pressed on my chest, making it hard to breathe.

My stomach was knotted in a fist of nerves, I had a lump in my throat and I felt like I was going to throw up. It wasn't a bug or anything, either. I had been feeling like this for the past while, the nausea only getting worse and worse. Because I was worried to death about Thomas. Worried that he was out there on the battlefield, injured, or worse. That explained why he hadn't been able to write me back. I was worried that he had somehow been captured by the Germans and was being held, and tortured for information.

Who knew what these Germans were capable of? I had heard the news, the stories about them sending people to camps as if they were spoils of war, and keeping them locked away from the world.

What if Thomas was locked up in such a terrible place?

But, even being locked up or worse, I couldn't help but think that it would be so much better if that were the reason for Thomas's silence, and not what really worried me.

Because what if Thomas had forgotten about me? What if he was perfectly fine, fighting for King and country, and he had merely decided that I wasn't worth his time and effort?

That would hurt so much more. That would be the real tragedy, worse than the war and the horrors that were taking place all over Eu-

MY SWEETHEART

rope. And that was what made my stomach turn. I had lost my appetite. I had lost so much weight, my clothes hung from my body like bags.

My parents thought my weight loss was due to the pressures and worries of war. After all, everything had gone pear shaped over the last nine months. It was now 1943, and even though the New Year had come with a bang, it hadn't been the kind we had been hoping for.

London had been bombed again. Flattened. The city was able to recover fairly quickly from an attack, but what had really been shattered was the wills of the people. Their faces had lost the lines of determination, instead replaced by creases of despair. And there were days when it felt like there was no hope left, not for a brighter tomorrow and not for the end of this terrible war.

I climbed out of bed, unable to lie down any longer. My worry and fear drove me, always pushing me to stay on my feet, to pace the house, to look out of the windows, as if I would see him walking down the road toward me. There were days where I caught myself searching for his face in the crowds around me, when we went to stand in the queues for rations.

Because the war had touched our home and my father's connections just as badly as it had touched everyone else. The luxuries were nowhere to be found and food was getting scarcer and scarcer by the day.

The house was quiet when I wandered through it. It was still early, the sun barely glancing over the horizon. The winter had been awful, but as spring crept in, the Earth tried to yearn for the beauty of summer with earlier daylight hours and warmer weather.

It was just a pity the beauty it yearned for was nowhere to be found anymore.

My father often stayed in his room until well after breakfast, and I didn't expect him to be around much these days. And my mother, well, it seemed as though she was getting sick. Not of anything particular, my father had asked a physician to see her. It was merely a case of her giving up.

And I understood it. The only thing that propelled me forward was the sliver of hope I clung onto, that Thomas was alive out there, and that by some miracle his heart still belonged to me.

I walked to the front door where the pile of mail had been put on the small table next to the coat stand.

Once upon a time, our butler Mr. Levine used to bring us our mail with our breakfast in the morning. But since the bombing, the staff had all fled and aside from the cook and one ladies' maid, we were without hope. And we filtered through our own mail.

I tasted my heart in my throat as I searched through the letters, looking for an envelope with Thomas's scratchy handwriting on it, one that would bring me a small point of light.

But there was nothing from him. As it had been for nearly eight months now.

My heart sank to my shoes. Despite knowing the odds, I still picked up the pile of letters every morning, hoping beyond hope that today would be different.

I took a deep breath and let it out in a sigh, trying not to let the worry eat me alive. My stomach twisted and turned, a swell of nausea overcoming me. I pressed my hand to my mouth. Was I going to throw up? It felt like it. I had thrown up from worry before, making my father worry that I struggled the same way my mother did.

But this was so very different.

When I walked through the breakfast room, planning a trip through the house to distract me from the thoughts of abandonment that plagued me, my father emerged from his room.

"Morning, dearest," he said, in a voice that sounded so infinitely tired. He always sounded tired these days. "Join us for breakfast?"

"Us?" I asked.

"Your mother is on her way down as well."

This was a rare occurrence. I couldn't remember when last we had eaten breakfast as a family.

"Why?" I asked.

My father looked drained, as if his very soul was tired.

"Because if we let the war get to us now, there will be nothing left of us in the end."

How right he was.

I nodded and sat down at the breakfast table, at my usual spot. I was in my nightgown, still. And my father wore his robe. The decorum, the uptight rules and regulations my father used to run this house by, had all slipped.

My mother entered and she, too, was in a robe and gown. Her cheeks were sallow, her skin pale, and her eyes had lost the life I had known them to hold before. She squeezed my shoulder in passing and sat down in her seat, as well.

The cook must have put the food on the table. It was a meagre meal of scrambled eggs and a small portion of potatoes. There was no more fresh bread, because half the ingredients could not be obtained anymore.

We ate in silence for a while and I wondered why we had done this at all.

"I hear that France is shooting down German planes left and right," my father said.

My mother looked up at him. "Do we have to discuss the war?"

My father continued as if she hadn't spoken at all.

"Despite the difficulty, the American troops are advancing as well."

Perhaps there was nothing else to speak of other than the war that had come to rule our lives.

"But the city will be bombed again, and it will happen sooner rather than later," my father said.

My mother nodded. She was agreeing, and I understood why. The city was falling apart. The Germans were managing to do what they had set out to do. The world was coming undone at the seams, and it was merely a matter of time before Germany would be able to take over without much of a fight.

"We need to leave town before that happens," my father said.

I snapped my head up at him and narrowed my eyes.

"Excuse me?"

"We are not safe here," he said. "And I have colleagues in the country who will be willing to house us. I wrote them and received word last week, by some miracle. The messenger had not been shot."

My stomach twisted violently and I put down my fork. If I left here, Thomas wouldn't be able to find me.

"We can't leave," I said.

My father frowned at me and my mother looked up, disturbed.

"If we stay here, we might die," he said.

"We can't just give up our home. What will become of it? What will become of us? It would be like surrendering."

"Darling, this is war. The only thing we should fight for is our lives. The rest can be replaced."

But it wasn't so simple. This was my heart we were talking about, the fact that Thomas wouldn't know where to start looking if he left. I had to stay here. I had to be here when he returned and came for me.

"I am not going," I said. "I won't."

"Be reasonable, Claire," my mother said.

"I am," I said. My fingers trembled. My whole body trembled, in fact. I couldn't leave here. It wouldn't only be leaving everything I knew behind, it would be leaving my future behind, too.

"You're not thinking clearly," my father said. "War is a difficult time and I know you're afraid. But I know what's best for this family. We'll be leaving as soon as we are able."

"You have no idea what's best for me!" I cried out.

My parents both looked at me in horror over such an untoward outburst. But my stomach lurched violently and I clapped my hand over my mouth and jumped up. I ran to the guest toilet and yanked open the door, throwing myself over the toilet bowl where I emptied the contents of my stomach.

My father had been right. If we let war get to us now, there would be nothing of us left. He had meant our family, but I was thinking of my hopes and dreams, the future I was holding onto.

And I was terrified that it was already too late.

Chapter 13

Thomas

We were in yet another small town—they all seemed the same and I had no idea what this one was called—when we were ambushed by a group of German soldiers. They had appeared out of nowhere, and attacked with viciousness we hadn't experienced in a while.

Most of the soldiers that we had encountered were as exhausted and malnourished as we were. But these seemed strong and they were serious about protecting their land, taking back what was theirs.

We did the best we could. I came face-to-face with a German soldier, too close to get in a good shot with the gun that was looped around my shoulder, and I had no choice but to engage in hand-to-hand battle.

But there was no way I was strong enough to take on this man who looked like he had been fed well for days and had more than enough sleep. How was it possible that the soldiers were in such good condition, when we were fading away?

I tried my best. I managed to get in a few blows, using my knife to cut where I could, but the soldier had the upper hand in no time. A blow through the face, one against the ear, and my world tilted on its axis. I fell to the ground, knocking my head hard and I saw stars.

Boots connected with my face over and over again, but a sharp pain in my ribs had me crying out. Despite the darkness that was starting to wrap itself around me, and consciousness that crept in quickly rather than slowly, I was aware that some damage had been done. I had been stabbed.

Judging by the way the pain numbed almost immediately, I knew it was serious. Flesh wounds hurt like all hell, but the ones that were really a problem could barely be felt.

I heard the fight raging on around me, felt the tremble of the earth as more bodies dropped next to mine, and I had a feeling that the Germans had the upper hand. We hadn't been strong enough to take them, and we had been taken by surprise, to boot.

Was this the end? Was this where I said goodbye to everything I had thought my future would hold?

I flashed on Claire, her picture perfect face and her blood red lips, the way her eyes changed when she looked at me. I imagined the sound of her laughter in my ears, and I ached for her. What if I never saw her again? And I had made her a promise that I would return for her.

Please, let me find my way back to her, I prayed to whoever would listen.

And then the blackness surrounded me completely, dragging me under and taking me away from the hell all around me.

But it didn't remain completely black. I was aware of moving. Of people speaking to me in urgent tones, and shouts a little further away. I was aware of being lifted and moved around, sometimes bumped so that I groaned and cried out.

But my thoughts and memories were interrupted by bouts of blackness, the darkness that swallowed me no matter how hard I fought against it.

I saw flashes of light, felt the breeze of the ocean against my face, the motion of waves rocking beneath me. Was the journey to the other side so long? Why did it take me so long to die?

And then I saw her face again. The woman I loved. Claire, my beautiful Claire. How I longed to touch her face again, to feel her soft skin beneath my fingers. How I wish I could see her one more time and tell her that I was sorry. Sorry that I couldn't make it back to her, sorry that I could not fulfil my promise of a life together.

And I wanted to tell her that I loved her, that she was the only thing that had kept me going for so long. I needed her to know what she meant to me, that even if she had decided I didn't mean anything to her anymore, she had still remained my world.

But when I reached out for her, she was just beyond my grasp, and she looked past me as if she didn't see me.

I was again aware of movement, being shifted from one flat surface to another. And then female voices surrounded me, soft and soothing, serious.

And then Claire was in front of me again, but this time, she was smiling at me. She sat next to me, reaching out and touching my arm. And to be touched by her again filled me with warmth and life that I had thought I had been drained of months ago. I looked into her beautiful eyes, getting lost in the magic that she held within them.

"You're going to get through this, Thomas," she said in that beautiful accent of hers. And I believed her.

Sometimes, I was aware that Claire was only a dream. I was aware that I was only conjuring her from my memories, creating the woman I loved to be right next to me so that I wouldn't slip back into the darkness.

And sometimes I was so sure she was real, I didn't know what the problem was, why we didn't just get up, her and I, and go home.

Because I was becoming aware that I was not dead, as I had thought. And I had to fight to be able to go home again. I had to fight whatever injuries were dragging me down, and I had to get back to what was important.

When I finally opened my eyes, I realized I was alive. And back in the real world.

I looked around, trying to figure out where I was. The room looked rich, with brown paneled walls, bookshelves. But hospital beds and curtains, too. Like a library or a home that had been transformed into a medical center.

These were created all over the place to care for the war victims.

"Excuse me," I said, and my voice was scratchy. I felt like I hadn't had water in a year. A nurse turned and hurried to me.

"You're finally awake," she said, the sound of her English accent, albeit a little flatter than I had heard out of Claire's mouth, made my heart sing.

"Where am I?" I asked.

"You're in hospital," she said. "We were worried you might not make it, being ripped apart like that."

The moment she said it, I felt the pain in my chest and I looked down. I wore no shirt and my chest was wrapped with white bandages.

"How bad was it?"

"A right gash, sir. It missed all the vital stuff, which is a miracle. But you lost so much blood we were worried. You're a fighter, you are."

She seemed in awe of me. And it was flattering, I suppose. But I needed to know where the hell I was. Had Claire been here? Had she come to see me, or had I dreamed it all?

"What city is this?" I asked.

"We are a couple of miles outside of London, sir. In Romford."

That wasn't too far away. But it wasn't in London. And I doubted Claire would know I was here. My heart sank when I thought of her face, feeling her next to me, pulling me through. It had been my own mind playing tricks on me, using her to get me through. Because no matter how much I was sure she had forgotten about me, she was still the only girl I would ever think of. She was the woman that had gotten me through, so far.

"How long was I out?"

"You've been unconscious for nearly a week, sir," she said.

A week?! What had I missed in that time? I doubted things had changed much with the war.

The nurse hurried away to help another patient and I lay my head back on the pillow, trying to relax. I hadn't asked how bad the injury had been. But judging by how I felt, and what she had told me so far, I wouldn't be sent home. They wouldn't send me back to the States because I wouldn't be unfit for battle.

Which meant that at some point, I would go back.

A part of me was sad at the idea that I would not go home to the rolling hills of my ranch in Montana. But the fighter in me wanted to get out there again. I wanted to show the bastards that it took more than that to take me down.

And I wanted to come back from this war and find Claire. I wasn't going to go back to Montana without her, I wasn't going to let go of something that I had known from the start was my destiny. Fate didn't hand you someone like Claire only to give up on it and walk away.

No matter what she felt or had decided over all these months, the only way I would stop chasing her was if I were dead.

I just needed to see her one more time before they sent me back. I needed to find her the moment I got out of here, and I needed to talk to her. She needed to know what I felt for her. And I needed to know what was going on, why I hadn't heard from her.

Maybe it had been the war. Times were tough, letters didn't make it. It happened to everyone.

But people also didn't make it, sometimes. I had heard no news from London, nothing about how things were going. And I worried that something might have happened to Claire, and that the war might have taken her away from me.

I worried that when I finally returned to find her, she would be gone.

Not getting letters from her had been hell. I had fought on with nothing but the memories of her touch, and her voice, in my mind. I had allowed our promise and the love I felt for her to drive me, because

I had nothing else. I had read the few letters I had received in the beginning so many times, I knew every word off by heart.

Where were my letters? Where were my personal affects? For a moment, I started to panic. I looked around frantically.

"Nurse," I called. "Nurse!"

Another nurse appeared, her face stern.

"You're not in pain," she said.

"Did my things come with me?"

She pointed at my bag on the floor against the paneled wall, dusty and dirty, a contrast against the rich wooden panel. But my aching heart was soothed and my breathed evened out again. I had panicked when I had thought that I'd lost Claire's letters.

It was all I had of her, all I could hold in my hands until I saw her again.

The last couple of months without any word from her had been hell and I needed that at least to pull me through until I could hold her in my arms again. Until I knew that I could continue fighting for her. Because no matter what happened, I didn't want to let go.

I didn't know what she wanted or where she was, where her head was when it came to me. But I knew that I wanted her by my side, that this war was just a stumbling block on our path to happiness. And if she still wanted me, then she was the woman I wanted to spend the rest of my life with.

Chapter 14

Claire

I wrote letters for Thomas every day, even though I was unsure he would receive them. Even though I was unsure that he wanted them. I had doubted myself so many times, telling myself that it was over, that he didn't care and wanted nothing to do with me.

But then, the moment I'd decided not to write him more letters, I started thinking about what it might be like to be injured, hungry and cold on the battlefield and to feel abandoned, too.

And I felt so guilty about believing that he would not fulfill his promises, that his words might not have been true, that I wrote another letter, and yet another.

I was sure that if he wasn't interested in me anymore, I would only be setting myself up for heartbreak. But I could recover from a broken heart, couldn't I? If he was still out there, yearning for me as I was for him, he deserved every second I did not give up on him.

When I woke up one morning, after I had searched the pile of letters at the door for a letter from him that I had known would not be there, I walked back to my bedroom. My father and mother had started eating together at the breakfast table again, but I often did not join them.

After my father's suggestion that we leave, and my little outburst that we had to stay, we barely spoke. I had nothing to say to him if he was set on taking me away from the home where Thomas would find me. And he was anxiously awaiting a reply from his contact that would house us, waiting for him to tell us it was time for us to leave to the country side.

I sat down behind my desk and reached for a sheet of paper. It was thick and smooth under my fingers, the cream paper beautiful to look at, so full of hope and possibility before any strokes of ink had been drawn upon it.

Slowly, I started writing a letter the same way I always did.

Dear Thomas, but I stopped. Something about this felt different. Something about this was... wrong.

I sat back in my chair and frowned at the letter I had started writing. I had never felt this way before. In all the months I had been writing Thomas, and with all the worry I had experienced, all the doubt and all the fear, I had never felt that something was different, that something had changed.

But this time, I knew in my bones that this letter would not reach Thomas where ever I thought he was. Somehow, I had a feeling that something had changed.

I stood and walked to my closet, choosing clothing to head out. I knew that my father would disapprove—the streets of London were anything but safe, now. But I had to get out, I had to find out what was going on.

As soon as I was dressed, I walked to the front door. Luckily, my parents had already finished their breakfast and neither of them were anywhere to be seen. I slipped out of the front door before my father could come to find me, hearing me walk through the house.

I didn't know where to start, but I knew that there were war offices close by and I headed in that direction. Perhaps they would know something, perhaps they could tell me where soldiers were being treated when they came back from the war. Because I had a feeling that something like that had happened. I didn't know how I knew, but I followed my gut.

And even though the war offices were terrifying, even though I hated the smell in the stale building and the war so evident on the faces of the people behind the desks, I found out what I needed to know.

Soldiers were being treated in Romford. If Thomas was anywhere, I knew that he would be there. Again, I didn't know how I knew, I just knew.

Travelling to Romford wasn't easy. The city was mostly blocked up, on lockdown, and the only people in the street were those looking for trouble or a way to survive after they had lost everything. The face of London had been transformed from a jewel that glittered in the sunlight to a scarred face, mottled with bruises. There was rubble everywhere, remnants of buildings that had crumbled during the bombing, broken furniture in piles and long shadows that still reached across the ground, searching for the darkness of night that was slowly being chased away by the rising sun.

Despite it being spring time, it felt like the sun was slow to rise, as if it too had lost all hope.

Finally, hours later, I arrived in Romford. I had covered most of the journey by foot. At the medical center, an old library that had been transformed, I found the list of names on the door. I ran my finger down the list, muttering the names. And then, by some miracle, I found him.

My heart leapt in my chest. And my stomach twisted with nerves. What if he didn't want to see me? What if he really had decided to move on?

Or what if he was so injured that I didn't recognize him? What if he didn't recognize me?

I shook my head. There was only one way I was going to be able to find the answers to all my questions, and that was by going inside and speaking to him myself.

When I walked into the building, I announced myself as Thomas's visitor. I had to sign a log, and then I was taken through to the recovery room. When I looked around at the beds, most of them filled with soldiers that had been injured, I was relieved to notice that most of them were in an agreeable state. This room was not for those in critical condition.

Which meant that Thomas would be conscious and recovering well.

I was relieved.

I looked around, trying to see if I could find him. And then suddenly, the moment my eyes locked with his, it felt like everything fell into place again. I was home.

"Claire?" Thomas asked, the disbelief on his face mirroring the shattered hope I had been feeling for the past couple of months. "Is that really you?"

I nodded and walked to his bed, slowly, checking myself. I wasn't quite sure I would be able to stop myself from doing something drastic if I moved any faster. When I stopped in front of his bed, I clasped my hands together in front of me.

"I was worried he was dead," I said.

Thomas shook his head. "I was worried you had forgotten about me."

Tears suddenly sprang to my eyes. He had been struggling with the same fears I had. And I couldn't hold back anymore. I hurried around the bed and threw myself at him, my arms around his neck, his arms closing around my waist. I heard him suck in his breath through his teeth and I was worried that I was hurting him, but when I wanted to pull away, he held tightly onto me.

"Don't let go," he said in a hoarse voice.

"I didn't," I answered.

It felt like we held onto each other for ages. We were making up for all the times we hadn't been able to reach each other, for all the latest letters we had written each other that had never arrived. When I explained to him that I wrote every day, he nodded.

"I knew my English girl wouldn't give up on me," he said, and put his hand on my cheek. I had missed his touch so much.

"Do you still want to come back for me when the war is over?" I asked the question that had been burning in my mind for months. "Do you still want me?"

"My darling girl, I don't think I could ever stop wanting you. You are the only thing that has gotten me through this war. And when it's over, I am going to whisk you away to the rolling hills, where there isn't a care in the world. I am going to show you a life where laughter and happiness is all that exists. Do I still want you? Claire, you have become my everything and I will never stop wanting you."

Tears rolled down my cheeks again and I closed my arms tighter around him. I couldn't believe that this was happening, that I had found him. I couldn't believe that after I had almost thought I should give up hope, I was right back in Thomas's arms again.

"Is there a way for us to slip out of here?" I asked.

Thomas looked around. "I am sure we can go for a walk," he said. "The nurses are very encouraging when it comes to physical exercise."

I nodded and Thomas flagged a nurse. After getting permission to walk around, he climbed out of bed. I noticed the bandages around his chest, and worried that he was in too much pain. But he shook his head when I asked.

"With you here, I feel no pain at all."

I took his hand, and together we walked toward the door. But instead of leaving the library through a back door that led to the gardens, Thomas tugged me towards stairs.

"There are rooms up there, offices transformed for the medical staff to live in. And they are empty during the day. Come with me."

"Are we allowed?"

"Of course not," Thomas said, with a twinkle in his eye. "But I need to be with you in every way possible, and I won't stand for rules that will affect who we are to each other."

MY SWEETHEART

Something in me lurched. This was exactly what I had hoped for when I saw Thomas again, being connected to him as we had been before.

I followed him up the stairs, and he closed us into the first bedroom we found. The desk had merely been pushed to the side to make way for a cot. But we had privacy, luxury didn't matter.

The moment we were closed in, Thomas pressed me against the door and kissed me with so much passion, as if he himself had invented kissing. And his hands roamed my body, touching every inch of me. I was on fire for him, I had yearned for his touch for months. And now that he was here in front of me, the heat that he built up with his hands and his mouth, and the fire that burned bright stretched between us, thin and elastic, and threatened to consume us.

We got rid of the clothes I wore, and the pants Thomas wore, the only piece of clothing on his body.

Then we tumbled onto the narrow cot together, naked and giggling. I was so in love with this man, the passion I had felt before as strong between us now as if we had never parted.

And when he slid into me, parting me, and stretching me until my body yielded, I looked into his eyes and saw the promise of our future together burning bright. He moved inside of me until I was reduced to nothing but atoms colliding, to a woman trembling with pleasure.

And when I came undone at the seams, so did he. When we orgasmed, we orgasmed together. And I knew that we would be connected, heart and soul, for as long as we were alive. This war could rage on, it could try to tear the world apart. But Thomas and I would forever be melded together. And we would get through the distance, until the time came that we would be with each other again.

I knew it the same way I had known that Thomas was here. I knew it the same way I knew that he loved me.

Chapter 15

Dane

I was on the road and in a mood. I was headed back to my Gran's house, away from Pinewood downtown, away from the police station. Hopkins could be such a dick. It wasn't like the chief didn't know what he had when I was on the force, I was one of the best officers in the damn station. But no, just because I had suffered a traumatic event and PTSD still rode me bareback sometimes, he believed that I wasn't ready to get back to work.

What the fuck else was I supposed to do? I was a police officer. It defined me. It was driving me crazy that I didn't have anything to do with my time. It had been months since I had been on the force, out on the street and making sure that everyone was safe. Hell, Pinewood was such a small place, nothing should have gone wrong in the first place.

But I guess tragedy could happen anywhere. It wasn't exclusive to big cities, and the shootout had gotten ugly because not everyone involved had known how to handle themselves.

When I thought back to it, I felt the tension in my shoulders, a headache that throbbed dully between my temples. And images flashed before me. Blood, so much of it, blossoming crimson on shirts. The smell of it in the air, metallic, awful. I could still taste it on my tongue, as if it was on my hands again.

The hollow feeling in my stomach opened up again and I felt like I was going to throw up. My chest was so tight I couldn't breathe. Dammit, I hated it when this happened. I couldn't even eat beef too rare these days, taste that afterthought of blood, without losing my shit like a child. As if I hadn't been someone who ran into the fray before, as if I hadn't been a hero.

Fuck, this was really eating me up. I hated that it ruled my life. I hated that because of some stupid accident, some stupid man with a gun, had screwed up my life this much. Someone else had made shitty decisions and now I was paying for it.

I tried not to focus on the past, on what had happened. On the memories. But the smell of blood was so thick in the car now, I couldn't breathe. I felt like I was going to throw up.

Roses, I thought about the roses. The smell of them. That I had to redirect my thoughts like that, with thoughts of an old woman's roses, disgusted me. It was pathetic.

I shook my head, trying to get rid of the images. Trying to get rid of the anxiety that crept in when I thought about it. At least my PTSD was a little more manageable now. Which was exactly why Hopkins had to leave feedback on the team. I couldn't sit and do nothing. How many days would I have to prune my grandmother's roses before I would lose my very identity?

There was a whole damn summer ahead and I had no idea what to do with myself.

PTSD. Hopkins had said that it was too much of a risk. What if I got into a situation that reminded me of that day? What if there was gunfire again? What if they teamed me up with someone else, and I lost it because it wasn't Pam.

Back. A risk. It made me sound pathetic. Everything I was centered around, was all about being strong, brave, and standing up for others. My entire existence was about serving and protecting. And now I was the one that apparently needed to be protected. It made me feel weak and I hated it.

By the time I pulled into my grandmother's estate, my mood was black and I had to focus to calm down. I couldn't see her like this, or speak to her in a way that was disrespectful. If I didn't reel in my emotions, I might have an outburst, and that would only prove Hopkins right.

And I wasn't going to do that. Because Hopkins wasn't right about me. I was more than capable of going back to work. I wish I had some kind of distraction. I needed something to throw my energy into, something that would take my mind off what had happened and my revised image of myself.

I climbed out of the car and walked to the main house. I glanced over the garden, looking at the roses. They were in full bloom and beautiful as ever. And in a short while, I would probably be out there again, pruning. Because no matter how ridiculous it was, it was the one thing that made me feel better.

The house was cool when I walked in through the French doors and I stopped in the hallway, listening for noise. The television was off and I didn't hear any sounds from the dining room. When I walked through the room, I couldn't find my Gran.

Eventually, I found her in her room, tucked into an old armchair with a blanket wrapped around her and on her lap. But she wasn't reading, she was staring out of the window and off in to the distance, her mind somewhere else.

"Hi, Nanna," I said, walking toward her. She didn't register that I was there, I had to call her twice before she slowly turned her head toward me. Her eyes were dazed, and she looked at me for a moment as if she was looking at someone else. She frowned slightly, and then she squeezed her eyes shut.

"Are you okay?" I asked, walking over and kneeling in front of her. She nodded and opened her eyes again, reaching out to me. I took her hand in both of mine.

"For a moment, I thought you were someone else."

"Who?" I asked.

But my Gran shook her head and turned it back to the window. I worried about her. These days, I felt like she was often somewhere else, her mind transported to a different place for a different time. But no matter how much I asked, she would never tell me what she was thinking about.

Finally, she looked back at me again, and her eyes bright, as if she were fully present again.

"How did it go at the station?" she asked.

I sighed and shook my head. "They don't think I'm ready."

Put her other hand over mine and patted it.

"All in good time, Dane. One day at a time, that's how you get through this."

I nodded, but felt some of my irritation creeping back in. "I'm just tired of waiting. There is nothing wrong with me, so I don't have to take things slow anymore. I just want to get back to what I'm good at. I want to matter again."

"My darling boy, you will always matter. Everything will happen in good time."

I didn't argue with her. There was nothing I could say to counter that, anyway. And I doubted she would understand. I appreciated that she supported and loved me, and that was all that mattered.

"Can I get you something?" I asked.

Gran shook her head. "What I need, unfortunately, no one would be able to give me."

I frowned. What did that mean? But my Gran patted my hand again.

"I think I need to rest."

I nodded, and stood. I let go of her hands and instead of quizzing her about what she meant, about where she was slipping away to, I left her room. I worried I was starting to lose her. My grandmother was getting old and since my grandad had passed away, she was going backwards by the day.

I worried what would happen to her, and where we would end up if this continued.

We were right here, the two of us.

Walking to the kitchen, I asked one of the servants to take my Gran a cup of tea in a short while, and then I headed out toward the rose garden. It was going to be another day filled with pruning, something that we keep me busy. With my fingers on the ground, at least felt like I was doing something. When I pruned the roses, I felt like there was proof. I could see the result of my handiwork. It was the only thing that made me feel remotely grounded again. It was therapeutic.

I was just getting into the pruning, whistling off tune, when a car loudly rumbled at the drive. I looked over my shoulder.

It was an old, rundown yellow beetle, not the sort of car that ever came to an estate like this. I frowned and turned a little, still sitting on my heels.

Inside the car, a young woman leaned across the seat, looking up at my Gran's house. Her face was riddled with curiosity, her eyes taking in the sheer size of the building and how immaculately everything was taken care of. She lifted a piece of paper, squinted at the contents, and looked up at the house again.

Who the hell was this woman?

I had to admit, she was gorgeous. Strawberry blond hair that hung over her shoulders, and bright eyes, although I couldn't tell what color they were. A mouth that was first in concentration, and a slender arm and hand casually thrown over the steering wheel as she leaned over to peer at the house.

It had been a long time since a woman had caught my attention like this. It had been a long time since anything but the damn roses had caught my attention.

She hadn't seen me until now. I was still kneeling between the roses, and her attention was on the house. I straightened myself out, pulled off the gloves I wore and dropped them on the ground. I wiped the sweat off my brow and walked toward the beetle. I wanted to know who this woman was and why she was here.

MY SWEETHEART

And curiously, I wanted to know what her voice would sound like when she spoke.

It was the strangest thing to think, but this woman, so out of place in her yellow beetle, with her beach-babe look, the intense concentration on her face, and the curious arrogance that made her think it was okay to be on the property without permission, all drew me like a magnet.

I walked toward the car.

After taking a couple of steps, her eyes flickered toward me. Surprise registered on her face and she sat back in her chair a little, glancing at the house and back at me again. Maybe she knew that she was on private property. Or something. I couldn't quite read her expression or her reaction.

And for some reason, that only intrigued me more. Who was this woman? What was she doing here?

I walked around the car so that I was on the driver side and she could wind down her window to speak to me. I waited for her to do exactly that. And the moment the window went down, the scent of her perfume wrapped around me. Floral, beautiful.

I took a deep breath and mentally had to check myself. This was just a woman, a stranger. What the hell was happening here?

"Who are you?" I asked, my voice sounding a lot snappier than I meant for it to, but at least it yanked me back to earth and away from whatever fucking dream world I was stuck in, or whatever spell she must have cast on me. This woman was mesmerizing and I had no idea why.

Chapter 16

Amelia

When I had spoken to Mrs. Mills about the Whiteside Guild, she had told me that the estate outside of town, the one with the roses, was the one where it was situated. I had been so excited.

But when I had driven out of town in my yellow beetle—the almost-antique car I had bought from Arthur's niece when she had moved out of town to study—I had realized that there were a couple of estates outside of town, and all of them had roses.

I had driven up and down the road where all the estates were situated, peering at the gate of every single one of them, looking for a sign that would indicate which was the Whiteside Guild, but none of them had been marked and I felt lost. Every time I thought I had found some kind of answer, it was another dead end. Was I ever going to find out what had happened to Claire and her Thomas?

Only one of the estates didn't have a gate that was completely shut, locking the property away from the world, so I drove up the driveway and toward the main house. It seemed wrong to be on this property with such a messed up car. My Beetle was an old model, not great but it got me around town just fine. But here, it seemed completely out of place.

Because the house on the estate was absolutely beautiful, extravagant and modest all at the same time. And the rose gardens were extensive. Immaculate. I leaned over the passenger seat and looked out of the window, trying to take everything in.

What was it like to live in a place like this? The people who lived here had to have such a different lifestyle, and I was fascinated by it. Imagine the history that was caught between those walls, the secret and the memories of days long gone.

Someone stood up from between the roses, and I jolted. I hadn't realized that someone had been there, watching me this whole time. I suddenly felt on the spot, aware that I was probably trespassing. I had let my curiosity get the better of me.

"Well done, Amelia," I said to myself and watched the man walked toward the car.

Damn though, he was hot. Like, super-hot. I knew I wasn't supposed to think about it like that—he was probably going to kick me off the property or report me for something, but I couldn't help but stare. He had eyes that seemed broody, an angular face, and he carried himself with pride when he walked toward me.

The closer he got, the more flustered I felt. I was hot under the collar and I suddenly wished that this piece of crap car had an AC system.

He wanted to speak to me, he wanted to berate me for being here. He was staring at me, his eyes so intense, it only made me feel even more flustered,

Quickly, I unwound the window to listen to what he would say. I couldn't tell him what I was doing here, there was no way. I had to think on my feet. But what the hell would I say? Just looking into his eyes made me feel like I would forget everything, even my own name.

And wasn't that just pathetic. He was a man. Just a man.

"Who are you?" He spoke in a snappy tone.

Shit, he was pissed off. And why not? I wasn't allowed to be here, I was sure. Places like this weren't exactly open for the public to come and ogle.

"I'm so sorry," I started. "I just—" I had to think fast. What did I just?

He leaned over a little to peer into the car, and that put his face considerably closer to mine. I could also smell his cologne, with an undertone of sweat, and heaven help me if that didn't make me feel weak at the knees.

What the hell was going on?

"I just absolutely love real estate," I blurted out. What the hell? Might as well go with it. "Pinewood has some of the oldest estates in the county, I heard. And I just couldn't stay away. I have to say, your gardens are beautiful."

The man lifted an eyebrow as if he didn't quite believe me.

"Thank you," he said curtly. "The house doesn't belong to me. It's my grandmothers. And it's her garden."

"Does she still live here?" I asked. My curiosity was eating at me. It was probably making me rude, too. I wanted to ask this man if his grandmother was Claire. Claire Whiteside, from the letter. I wanted to know if I had found the right estate, or if she lived in one of the others.

Was this the woman who had written the letter? What would she do if I showed her? Would she tell me about it? I wished that I could see her, and speak to her, hoping I could offer her the physical remnants of a beautiful memory. I wondered if it would make her happy, or break her heart.

And I was obviously getting away from myself. The man was still staring at me as if I was crazy, and I had to pull myself together. I couldn't keep focusing on the scenarios in my mind. I have thought of so many different ways that I would have broken the news to Claire that I had found her later, I had thought of a million questions that I wanted to ask.

"May ask what your intention is with my grandmother?" the man asked.

Of course, I sounded like a crazy stalker. A psychopath.

"I just wanted to find out if she is Claire Whiteside, the woman who started the Whiteside Guild. You know—the roses?"

I felt like an idiot. I probably sounded like one too.

But then, for some unknown reason, the man smiled at me. And damn, did that take my breath away. If I had thought he was handsome before, he was drop-dead gorgeous now.

"You are quite pushy, aren't you?" he asked.

I blushed. "I don't mean to be. I just... I get carried away."

He chuckled. Why was this so amusing? I wasn't sure if I liked the angry person, better. The truth was, I was relieved that he saw humor in this. But when he smiled at me, I felt off balance. I felt like my knees were going to buckle. And I wasn't even standing.

"My name is Dane," he said, holding out his hand. I hesitated for just a moment before I took it.

"Amelia," I said, introducing myself, too.

His hand was large, and strong. Calloused. This was a man who used his hands often, and there was something very attractive about it. I didn't like men with soft hands.

I looked into Dane's eyes, and my stomach did a little flip. He was extremely attractive. I was going to have to work really hard to think straight with him around.

"Are you a visitor? Passing through?" Dane asked. I wanted to point out that it was unfair that he was asking me questions without answering the ones I had asked. But I was trespassing on private property, and he was the grandson of the owner, not even just a gardener, so I probably didn't have a foot to stand on.

"No, actually, I live in town," I said.

Dane frowned. "That's interesting. I haven't seen you around. I would have remembered if I did."

Was that a compliment? I wasn't sure.

I pulled up my shoulders. If he lived tucked away in a house like this, I didn't blame him.

"I haven't been here for long, I only moved to Pinewood a short while ago. I work at the antique shop."

He laughed. I wasn't sure if it was a mocking laugh, but the sound of his voice was incredible. Deep, silky smooth. I wanted him to laugh again just so that I could listen.

"In all the years I have lived in Pinewood, I have never set foot in there. Does it do it for you?"

All right, this was where I drew the line. It was one thing to try to find out who I was because I was trespassing, but it was quite another to get so personal. I owed this man nothing, unless it was an apology for being somewhere I wasn't allowed to be.

"I need to get going," I said, clearing my throat. "It was nice to meet you, Dane. Once again, the house and the gardens are beautiful."

He nodded and took a step back. It was as if he shut down, becoming a little more reserved again. I was fascinated by the way that he had the capacity to open up and then close down in the blink of an eye.

"Thank you for stopping by, I guess," he said.

Was that sarcasm? I couldn't read this man. I didn't know why that flustered me even more. He was just a man, living on an estate outside of town. A very, very hot man. But that didn't matter.

"Will I see you around?" he asked.

I looked at him, blinking. It was a strange thing to ask someone he had just met. But somehow, the idea that he wanted to see me again made my stomach lurch. Of course, he might just be being polite. Although, that was a very different sort of kindness.

For a moment, I wondered what I was going to say. How did I respond to something like that?

Luckily, my years as a personal assistant—dealing with difficult clients where I always had to put on a beautiful face and a welcome smile—came to my rescue.

I offered him a bright smile, the same kind of smile I had always offered everyone in the business world, and pulled up one shoulder.

The latter was possibly a little flirtatious.

"I am sure you will. After all, that's how small towns work, right?"

He laughed and it was that same deep, rich tone.

I had to get out of here. If I didn't leave now, I might want to stay. And that was just ridiculous, considering that I didn't know this man at all. And I was clearly not very welcome.

I threw my car into reverse and backed out of the drive without looking at Dane again. As soon as I turned onto the road, I rolled up my window and headed toward Pinetown. I was mortified. What had that conversation been? Something about Dane and the way he had responded toward me had me unsettled.

And what was worse, I hadn't found out anything about Claire Whiteside and whether or not that had been her estate. All I knew was that the estate had a man who was incredibly handsome.

But I wasn't going to think about that. I had to think about the letter, about my mission. I had to think about Claire and what I would do next to find my answers.

Because I still wanted to know where she was, and how I could contact her. I needed to know if she had ended up with Thomas, if their love had been realized, and if she had lived happily ever after. I couldn't leave these questions answered, not now.

I drove back to Pinetown, thinking about the letter and about Claire and about everything else I was going to do to find my answers, anything to take my mind off Dane. I didn't know what it was about him that had created such an impression. And I wasn't even going to acknowledge the strange feeling in my gut, something that felt almost like butterflies. Like nervousness.

Or like bad food. What did that say about a man, if I couldn't even figure out what I felt around him?

I shook my head as if I could shake off the thoughts. I really had to stop thinking about this now.

Chapter 17

Claire

It had been three weeks since I had seen Thomas at the hospital. We were still in London, despite my father's wishes that we leave the city. His colleagues in the country hadn't answered his letter, despite sending several more, and we were starting to think that the safe house that had been arranged for us was a dead end. My father seemed to have fallen into a slump after that. And my mother had withered away more and more.

But I walked with my head in the clouds.

We hadn't had much time together in Romford. I hadn't been able to sneak out of the house again to see him—after leaving the first time my father had been furious. I had been gone for hours.

And then, Thomas had recovered and been sent back to the front.

I had been heartbroken, if I had to tell the truth. I had felt as though Thomas had been returned to me, only to be ripped away again. But at least, after we had slept together that day, we had taken the time to explain to each other exactly what had happened. I had told him that I had written him letters every day. And he had told me how he hadn't received any of them since the first few, and how he had been worried that I had given up on him, that I had moved on.

He had experienced the same fears that I had, worried that the other didn't feel the same about the promises we had made.

But while we had been together in Romford, we had confirmed our promises to each other. I would wait for Thomas, until the end of time, so that he could come back for me and whisk me away to Montana

MY SWEETHEART   113

where we would live happily ever after. After the horrors of war, such a happy ending was what we both deserved.

And now that I knew that Thomas still felt the same about me, I could breathe easier.

But only just. Because war was still raging on, and there was still a chance that Thomas would be injured again. He had been lucky, this time. It had been a miracle that he had not been killed.

One morning, I started throwing up. At first, I had thought it was a stomach bug, or something I had eaten. Or perhaps the worry that Thomas would not be safe out on the battlefield, and that I would never see him again. Throwing up during the day had become something that had happened more often, especially during the time where I had worried that I wouldn't see Thomas again.

As a result, my father had not looked at it too closely, either.

But I had known that something was wrong. Something was different than it had been before. And it wasn't very long before I had connected the dots.

I was pregnant. With Thomas's child. It was far too early to tell. Far too early to show. Often, women only found out after two months or so. But I just knew that I was with child, with Thomas's child. I didn't need a physician or to wait for my monthly cycle not to arrive.

And somehow, despite the terrible timing of it all, I couldn't find it within myself to be unhappy about it. To carry a piece of Thomas with me wherever I went... it seemed like an answer to my prayers.

A week after figuring it out, I went into town to see a physician. I needed to verify, to be sure. But when the physician confirmed that I was with child, it was only a verbal affirmation of what I already knew. So, after seeing the physician, I did not go immediately back home. Instead, I walked to Ruth's house.

The Allen's still lived in the same house they always had, just as we did. And even though Margaret and Dorothy had both left town, I still had someone I could turn to.

When Ruth and I were in the parlor at her home, locked away from her family so I was sure that our conversation would not be overheard, I confided in her.

"What?!" She cried out. "Claire!"

"Don't look at me like that," I said. "Did you think I was going to stay away from him after how I felt? Our union only made sense."

"Well, it didn't make a lot of sense if you are pregnant, now. We are in the middle of the war. How are you expecting to raise a child? Who knew how long this war will continue. This isn't the kind of life you want to bring a child into, not now."

I pulled up my shoulders. Of course, I understood what Ruth was saying and the thought that this was a terrible place to bring a baby into the world had crossed my mind several times. But I couldn't change fact—I was pregnant.

"What is it you expect me to do? I am very serious about Thomas, and I want to raise this child."

"But suppose you will have to do it alone?" Ruth said. "What are you going to do?"

I had thought about that, too. And I had to admit that the idea of losing Thomas and having to raise this child alone did scare me. I had no idea how I would do it. But I knew that I was determined enough to find a way. That had already become apparent in so many different situations.

"Do you know where he is?" Ruth asked.

I shook my head. Thomas and I had resumed writing letters to each other the moment he had left Romford, but again, most of our letters didn't reach each other. I had managed to get one through to him, and a reply had found me weeks later. But other than that, there had been nothing.

"I know that he's safe, though."

"How do you know?" Ruth asked.

I couldn't answer her. I just knew that he was alive. The same way that I had known that he had been injured and he wouldn't receive the letter I had been trying to write. The same way that I had known I would find him when I had set out to Romford, covering most of the journey on foot. The love I felt for Thomas transcended everything—the laws of physics, the concept of time and place, and sometimes reality itself, it seemed. And I knew that no matter what, Thomas and I would be reunited again.

"You can't do this on your own, Claire," Ruth said. She kept her voice low, as did I. Because even though we were both sure we would not be bothered, this was not the kind of conversation you wanted any of your family members to overhear.

"And why not?" I asked.

Ruth rolled her eyes at me. "Don't pretend like your life is that easy. The war has touched all of us, and I don't think your father will agree with anything of it. If he knew—"

"Which he won't."

"What do you think he's going to do when you tell him? He will put two and two together, you know. And he might very well disown you. What will you do for money, then?"

Of course, Ruth was right. My father was immensely upset with me half the time already. So the chances of him disowning me were good. It was a scandal for me to be pregnant, especially his circle of society. And it was in the middle of the war, when bringing a child into the world was a difficult thing.

But my father had controlled me my entire life. He had controlled my mother. And look where that had brought us—my mother was waltzing away and I was breaking the rules behind my father's back. His system wasn't working.

Maybe being out of that house, free to do what I wanted, wouldn't be the worst thing.

Ruth and I talked about it for a little longer, but she could offer me no useful advice, and after getting it off my chest, I didn't want to speak about it anymore. I was worried about being pregnant, scared to do it without Thomas. But I wasn't going to go into that with Ruth. I didn't feel like she understood what I felt for him.

No one understood, no one but Thomas himself.

Once our visit was finished, I walked back toward my own place. But I took a bit of a detour, ending up a few blocks away outside The Bell. It was closed, now, the windows boarded up and the door permanently shut. It had been for some time.

But despite how everything had been tainted by the war, it would not ruin the memories.

This was where I had met Thomas first, where I had locked eyes with him when he had walked through the door. It felt like it had been in a different lifetime, but even now, so far removed from it all, I remembered how my stomach had lurched when his eyes had locked on mine, how I had known that I had to go and speak to him, no matter what.

When someone like Thomas crossed your path, when you found a love like that, you did everything to keep it.

I walked on toward home. My mind was filled with images of Thomas, of memories. I flashed on the way he looked at me when we made love. The way he touched me, the way our bodies came together until we were one.

I thought about the way that we had conversations, how I felt like we could talk about anything. And how our dreams were aligned.

Thomas was still with me everywhere I went. I thought of him every minute of every day. Every breath that I took was filled with a prayer that he was still alive, that he would come home to me. I was waiting for him, and I would wait for him until he returned.

It was all my life had become.

MY SWEETHEART

But I knew that I was not wasting my time. I knew that Thomas was still alive. And I knew that as long as we were both breathing, we would find each other. There was no way that we could be kept apart. My heart belonged to him, and his to me. And we were going to find a way to be together despite the war, despite the difficulties with my family, and despite the distance that separated us.

The waiting would not last forever. The war would end, eventually. Thomas would return to find me, and he would take me back home. And when he did, we would turn our backs on this difficult time and we would only look forward. We would spend our every waking minute together, and we would live happily ever after.

Thomas, me, and this baby that we would raise together.

It was with happy thoughts like these that I continued home, not even noticing the damage that the war has done to the city. When I focused on my future, on how happy I would be and on what I was waiting for, the pain and the suffering all around me fell away. The war raged somewhere in the distance, and I walked with my feet firmly planted on a path that would take me toward my destiny.

Because that was the very definition of love, wasn't it? The promise that everything would be all right, and our lives would be whole again. It was the promise that I would be reunited with my other half, and he with me.

And then, hand-in-hand, we would walk into the sunset, together.

Chapter 18

Thomas

I couldn't say that I wanted to be back out in the field, that I wanted to have a rifle in my hands again and trudge through mud looking for a fight. I would much rather have stayed with Claire, to build a life with her. Seeing her in Romford had reminded me just how much she meant to me, and how much I ached for her when we were apart.

But my injuries had healed enough for me to be able to go out into battle again, and the war wasn't over. They needed every able-bodied man to fight, and I wasn't going to be a deserter.

It had been three months since I had seen Claire, since I had held her in my arms and told her that I loved her. After having seen her again, the past three months had seemed almost harder than the year before that.

But we had confirmed our promises to each other, declared our love again. And now I knew that when the war was over, Claire would definitely be there waiting for me. And it put so much hope in my heart, and that I knew I would stay alive and find a reason to get back again.

I had to get back to London to find the piece of my heart that was missing when we weren't together.

We were in a small building outside a town in Poland, ready to infiltrate. We had received word that the town had been terrorized by the Germans, and a lot of the locals were being held hostage.

"We have to get in fast and make quick work of it, gentlemen," our team leader said. "The element of surprise is the only thing we have going for us. The Germans are machines."

We all nodded. He was right, of course. I didn't know how it worked, but the Germans seem to have the upper hand in every fight. It was as if they had the best food and the best training, while we were left with nothing. I didn't know how it was possible.

But we had to free those hostages. We had to save as many lives as we could.

I rubbed my chest where the knife had wedged between my ribs. The gash had been a terrible one when I had seen it under the bandages, and I myself had been surprised that I was alive.

The wound had healed well enough, I was able to fight without difficulty most of the time. But sometimes, the pain returned in waves and I felt uncomfortable, the burning sensation shooting into my lungs.

"How are you doing?" Harry asked, kneeling next to me. Somehow, we had managed the luck of finding each other. I hadn't thought that I would see him again once I had been taken away for medical attention. And he had believed that I had lost my life.

But as with Claire, faith had brought me back to the people that were important, and I was glad to see my friend again.

"I'm perfectly fine," I lied. Because I wasn't going to allow something like this injury to hold me back. I was alive, and for that I was grateful. And I would do everything in my power to get back to Claire. This war was nothing more than a stumbling block.

"We're going to nail them," Harry said, when we prepared ourselves.

I nodded. We were going to get in there, take care of business, and get out.

We were silent as we left the building where we had met for our orders, and as we crept closer to the town, I could feel the tension balled around me. Everyone was nervous. It was one of those cases where no one knew if they were going to walk away alive. Every battle during the war was a question. Nothing was certain.

My stomach turned with nervousness. When I glanced at Harry, he had sweat on his brow. But our rifles were lifted and ready, and I tapped the knife on my hip, making sure that I knew exactly where it was. Because the moment we were in the fray, there would be no time to think, only to act.

We crept into town, but it seemed deserted. A few of us went through the first houses, but they were empty. Something was wrong.

We met at the center of town, the soldiers all looking as confused as I felt.

"Maybe we got the wrong information," Harry said.

But before someone could answer, the terrible noise surrounded us, the sound of hundreds of men shouting and bullets started flying around us. We had to duck and cover immediately, and in the blink of an eye, we were in the middle of a war zone.

Harry and I both found cover behind a wagon that had been tipped on its side. Bullets bit into the wood all around us, and I knew that if we stayed here, we were not going to survive for long.

"Get to that car over there!" I shouted above the ruckus of the bullets. "I'll cover you!"

I leaned around the side of the wagon and started firing shots, giving Harry a chance to crawl across the ground and make it to the car. At least it was more bullet-proof, and safer than the wooden wagon.

Harry did the same, firing shots to cover me and I joined him.

"This is a slaughterhouse, they must have known we were coming," Harry shouted.

Before I could answer, a German soldier jumped over the car and onto Harry. They scuffled on the floor, guns being kicked away and knives were drawn. I kicked the soldier off Harry and shot him. I saw the way his face exploded into a blossom of blood in front of me and I felt sick to my stomach. The first few times I had killed people, I had thrown up. It wasn't as bad anymore, but I would never get used to it.

"Thanks," Harry said, and when I looked at him, he had blood spattered on his face.

I nodded. There was no time to rest. We jumped back into the fight and the battled raged on, though the conditions worsened. The sun had disappeared behind the clouds as if it didn't want to see the bloodshed. The wind picked up and a chill grew in the air, the presence of death all around me.

Focusing on Claire, her lips and her eyes, I allowed her to take me away from the pain and the suffering and the death that I saw all around me.

I attacked Germans that were close to me, firing to kill, managing most of them. When Germans attacked me, the soldiers jumping onto me and trying to take my life, I drew my knife and managed to defend myself. Harry and I fought side-by-side, and as a team we could work better, faster.

But it wasn't something to celebrate. Our teamwork kept us alive, but took the lives of so many.

I tried not to think about the effects of war, how it worked that people who would have been innocent under other circumstances were now forced to become murderers.

"Thomas!" Harry cried out and I spun around to see the German on him, slamming him in the face, using the butt of a rifle. Harry's face was almost unrecognizable in seconds. I ran toward the soldier, letting out an animalistic cry and I jumped onto his back. I pulled my rifle around the soldier's throat, squeezing as hard as I could to cut off his air. The soldier fought, clawing at me, trying to get the rifle off his neck so he could breathe. But I had an anger inside me, a fury. Harry was my best friend, the only friend I had at the moment, and he needed to be protected.

After a while, the soldier slumped in my arms and I knew that he was dead. And with that, the terrible feeling of nausea and disgust rolled over me. I leaned to the side and threw up.

I scrambled on the ground to get to Harry and I shook him.

"Harry, are you okay?"

Harry didn't respond. His face was a mess, his bones crushed and everything was bloody. It was matted into his hair as well.

I shook him again. "Harry, it's no time to sleep on the job."

That had been a joke we shared during training, when we had been so tired we hadn't been able to think straight. But Harry wasn't sleeping. The blows had been enough to end it for him.

Harry was dead.

The moment I realized that, I threw up again. I retched until there was nothing left in my stomach—not that there had been anything in it to begin with. And after dry heaving for a while, I started shivering. The war still raged on around me, people shouting, and people dying. But I was stuck in a bubble where my best friend had just been killed, and I didn't know which way to go.

"Thomas, you have to get up and keep fighting," one of the other soldiers on our team said, suddenly next to me. I looked up at him, unsure what to say. How did he know that I could? What if this was the end for me, too. How could I keep doing this? Until now, I had managed. War was awful, but I had been able to deal with it. But now? It suddenly felt like too much.

"If you give up now, you're going to die. Get up and fight. If not for you, then for the people you love."

That did it. It snapped me out of the shock that I had fallen into when I had discovered Harry's death. I had to fight to get back to Claire. I had promised her that I would come home to her, and fetch her and take her to Montana with me. I couldn't afford to be killed on the battlefield because I was frozen by my sorrow. I had to get up and fight, I had to stay alive. I had to do everything in my power to go home to her, so that I could give her the life she deserved.

Because she didn't deserve me dying the way Harry did. She deserved me alive and well so that I could take care of her. And I had to get out of here. Away from the bloodlust, away from the anger and hatred, away from the pain.

But the only way forward, was through it.

So I picked up my gun, collected ammunition from Harry's dead body and took his knife. I looked at my friend one more time, a quick tribute to the life he had lived, and I turned my back on him. I threw myself into the battle with a rage I hadn't felt before, shooting Germans so that they dropped like flies, attacking with my knife and hacking into pieces.

At some point, it felt like this war was never going to end, we were going to battle the Germans until the dead of night.

But then, eventually, the few that survived ran away. And a handful of us stood between the dead bodies and blood, breathing hard, disbelieving that it was over.

When I looked around me, I knew that it wasn't over, though. Yes, we had won this fight. But the war wasn't over. And even when it was, years from now, these images would haunt me. It would never really be over for me, would it?

No, I knew that the only thing that would get me through, the only thing that would suit me from now until eternity, was having Claire by my side and living a life that was free of pain. I wasn't only going to go home to save Claire from the suffering of war. After this, when I finally made it out and we were back in Montana, I would be saving myself, too.

Chapter 19

Dane

I couldn't stop thinking about her. I didn't know what the hell it was—I had met so many women in my life and they were completely inconsequential. But the memory for some reason stuck around and every now and then, I caught myself thinking about her. The quirky woman in the old Beetle, who had made excuses as if she thought I would believe them. Whatever she had been doing on our property, it hadn't been because she liked real estate so much.

I wasn't an idiot.

But her bright smile had captured me, and I wanted to see her again. And what was so wrong about that? It was good for me to keep busy, to make friends, to be distracted from my own thoughts.

So, a week later, I found myself wandering into the antique shop in town. I had always thought the shop was the stupidest thing ever. Why would you want to hold onto the past? Why would you want to look back when you could move forward? I didn't understand people who traveled all over the country to find antiques that had once belonged to someone else once upon a time. If you thought about it, everything belonged to someone once upon a time, unless it was brand-new. They were many things that could be considered nostalgic if you really wanted to go that route.

I wasn't the sentimental type, and I didn't understand it.

Now, walking into the shop, I was again struck by how pointless it seemed. There were objects all over the place, packed neatly and it had obviously been done with care and attention. I looked at some of the items, waiting for Amelia to come and assist me. The bell above the door had announced my arrival, after all.

As I walked through the merchandise, I looked at the different objects—cutlery sets, old china, pictures in dusty frames, chests, jewelry boxes and even music boxes. I would never buy any of these things, I thought.

After a while, I wandered deeper into the shop, looking for her.

The door stood open a crack, and I could see movement behind it. I pushed it open slowly, aware that this wasn't the part of the shop, but she was there. She stood hunched over an old Globe, that same look of concentration I had seen at the estate riddling her face.

And, she was just as beautiful now as she had been then.

I cleared my throat and she jumped. When she saw me, she laughed nervously. It was cute to see her flustered like this.

"Oh! Dane. I'm so sorry, I didn't hear you come in."

I shook my head. "May I?" I gestured into the room, asking if I could come in.

Amelia looked around before she nodded. "I'm afraid it's a bit of a mess. This isn't usually open to customers."

"Don't worry, I'm not a customer. This isn't quite my scene."

"Then why are you here?"

I blinked at her for a moment, wondering if I should answer. But instead, I turned my attention to the globe and nodded at it. "What's that?"

Amelia's eyes turned to the Globe and they sparkled with interest.

"It's an old globe, with the towns and lay of the land before it was divided up into Germany and France. Look at this, you can see how the borders were changed to become the countries they are now. And these towns," she pointed them out, "I wonder if they still look the way they did back then."

I could tell how much of a passion she had for her work. I didn't care about antiques at all. But she was so intrigued by it, so caught up.

And the passion and interest was beautiful on her. It made her eyes shine, it made her face come to life, and her smile golden.

"It seems to be in good condition," I said. I didn't know shit about antiques, but I could see that, at least.

"Very good, this will go for a lot."

"Do you mean price?"

Amelia nodded at me. "I have to put a price on everything to sell it. But to be honest with you, I think that every piece in the shop is priceless. How can you possibly want to put a price tag on the memories that come with it? How can you even begin to add words to what this must have meant to someone once upon a time? I always wonder how these things end up in my shop."

"Is this your shop?" I asked.

Amelia looked up at me and blushed. "No, I don't own it. I just work here, for Arthur. I'm sure you know him?"

I nodded. I did know the weird old man. Of course, this would be his place. I should have put two and two together.

"Anyway, I like to think of it as my shop because I feel so at home here."

I couldn't keep my eyes off her. Everything about her was beautiful, from the way that she spoke, to the way that she thought about things, to the way that she was interested in things that really didn't matter. She was mesmerizing.

"We should probably get back into the shop," Amelia said, pushing the globe backward carefully.

I nodded, and stepped to the side to let her walk through first. I followed her and she walked to the counter.

"Is there something I can help you with? Were you looking for something?" Amelia asked. Because I hadn't answered her when she had asked me what I was doing there.

"Go out with me tonight," I blurted.

She looks up at me, surprised.

"You're not here to buy an antique," she said. A statement, not a question.

I shook my head. "I'm here to see you. I was wondering if you wanted to go out with me."

There, that was a lot better. I didn't sound like such a damn fool.

"Tonight?" Amelia asked.

I nodded. "What time do you get off?"

She looked at me for a long time, color creeping onto her cheeks. She was even more beautiful when she blushed. How was that possible?

"Six," she said.

"Six it is."

In a town as small as Pinewood, they weren't a lot of restaurants to choose from. But there were still a few that were decent, and I had chosen to take Amelia to Oregano, one of my favorites. It wasn't the best restaurant in terms of stars, but it made the best food and I loved the atmosphere.

When I returned to her shop at six, she was ready to go out. I had told her that she didn't have to worry about changing for the date, and I had made sure that I was dressed casually, too. Jeans, a collared shirt with the sleeves rolled up, sneakers.

I had made an effort to look good. But Amelia? She didn't have to do anything at all. I had seen her earlier that day, but when I looked at her now, it was as if I saw her for the first time yet again. Her strawberry blond hair was pulled back in a half up ponytail, and her eyes—a brilliant green—stood out with a little smoky eyeshadow. Had she wore the make-up, earlier? I liked to think that she might have applied it for my sake.

But I wasn't going to be an arrogant prick and assume that she was as attracted to me as I was to her.

She wore simple jeans and a tank top, with a sheer blouse over it, and sandals. And she looked beautiful. Her lips were rosy pink and I wondered what they would taste like.

Focus, Dane, I scolded myself.

"I haven't actually been here," Amelia said, when we were seated at Oregano.

"No? How long have you been in town?" I asked.

"Not that long, and seeing that it's just me, there is no reason to go out. It's easier to get takeaways."

I should have asked her if she was involved with someone. But maybe if she was, she wouldn't have accepted my date. I was relieved, either way, that she didn't have anyone.

"I grew up here," I said. "This place is like a second home to me. I used to come here with my grandparents all the time."

I could see Amelia's curiosity flair when I spoke about my grandparents. What was it that she wanted with my grandma? I knew that she had come to the estate for a reason, but I didn't know what it was. Still, I didn't want to pry. I had a feeling that if I asked questions, she was going to shut down on me and feed me another bullshit line. Maybe, if I gain her trust a little bit, she would tell me.

"I grew up in New York," Amelia said.

That captured my interest. "Why on earth would you move to a small town like Pinewood, then?"

Amelia pulled up her shoulders. "When you live in a big city, you become someone without an identity. At least, that was how it felt to me. I was just another person, a face disappearing in the crowd. My job wasn't my job because of my ability to do it well, it was because they needed someone and I happened to be in the right place at the right time. If it hadn't been me, it could very well have been someone else and no one would have cared about the difference. In a place like Pinewood, people matter because of who they are. And I like that."

It was a very different way of looking at things. I hadn't thought about it that way. I had gone to the city a couple of times and I had always been impressed by how amazing it seemed, how luxurious and distracting.

"I just think it's interesting because people usually run away from places like Pinewood to escape to places like New York, not the other way around," I said.

Amelia pulled up her shoulders. "I guess I'm not like everyone else."

No, that was the statement of the century. Amelia was nothing like the other women I had met. Everything about her intrigued me. She was beautiful, but in an unassuming way. And she was interesting, but she had no idea how much. The way she looks at the world was so different, through rose tinted lenses, when I only saw the harsh reality.

We started talking about work, and she explained to me how she had been a personal assistant once before, and how much she enjoyed being the shop manager here.

I told her about being a police officer. But I didn't mention the shooting, the fact that I had been benched for a while. I didn't want her to think less of me. I wanted to impress her, because I couldn't get enough of the attention she was giving me. Just being the person she directed her attention to when she told me something felt like an honor.

And I wanted more of that.

It had been a long time since I had thought about being with someone again. I'd had a few girlfriends, but no one serious and then I had become caught up in my work and that had taken over everything else. But now, with Amelia opposite me, I found myself thinking about dating again. It was very early to be able to think about something like that, but Amelia was so different and she really drew my attention.

Was this something that could go somewhere if I let it? Was she someone that I could pursue? I hoped so, because when you met someone who drew your attention the way Amelia did, you did something about it.

Chapter 20

Amelia

Going out on a Friday night hadn't been in the cards for me. I had never really been someone to go out and mingle, my work had kept me too busy in New York, and now that I lived in Pinewood, I enjoyed being home and just spending time by myself. I had never really spent enough time doing things that I wanted, and now that I was able to, I liked being an introvert.

Usually, I spent time reading historical romances, or researching facts that I had come across at the shop. Or I watched old movies.

So, when Dane had asked me out on a date, it was even more out of the ordinary for me. I hadn't come to Pinetown with the idea in mind to find someone to connect with. Not like this. And definitely not someone so attractive—was it even legal for someone to be as hot as he was?

I laughed inwardly at my pathetic joke.

But the date really was going very well. Dane was a perfect gentleman. He had come to collect me at the shop, dressed casually but well put together and he had opened the car door for me, and everything. At the restaurant, he had pulled out my chair for me, and he had taken the liberty to give the waiter my order when I had decided what I wanted to eat.

Spending time with Dane was refreshing. I was used to assholes, and to have someone like Dane treat me like I was worth something was new.

I had to admit, when he had found me in the storage room at the shop, he had caught me off guard. That he had come to find me there had been so flattering. And then he had showed interest in what I was looking at, even though it was clear that he had never really cared about history.

I liked that about him—that he could be interested in the things that I liked, even though it might not be something that made him tick. He reached out to me, tried to understand me on some level. It was very rare for a man to be anything other than self-centered. Maybe I was stereotyping, but it was all I had known while I had dated in New York.

When I had seen Dane at the estate, I had thought he was a gardener. He had been busy with the roses, standing up out of nowhere. And then I had found out that he was the grandson of the estate owner, and that had changed everything for me.

But now, Dane was down to earth. Human. And that changed everything again. I actually really enjoyed spending my time with him. I was surprised by how well we got along, how we seemed to be compatible even though we had very different interests.

And I was surprised by how often I laughed during our date. When he spoke, even about the silliest things, he was so funny. He said things in a way that just caused me to crack up. I couldn't remember when last the man had made me laugh like this.

"I still don't understand how someone like you, the woman who had it all, could leave New York City behind for the slow-paced life here in Pinewood," Dane said.

I had explained to him how I had fallen away in New York, how I had found that the person I was just wasn't being noticed.

"I think it's very simple," I said. "I started losing my identity. My whole life consisted of work. And it wasn't even work that would propel me in a direction that would be worth it one day. It was work for someone else. Work that would get someone else somewhere one day.

And where would that leave me? At one point, I realized that no matter how hard I worked, how many hours I put in, I would never reach any goals of mine. And that isn't alive, is it?"

Dane shook his head. "No, I suppose it isn't. But it's a very different way of looking at things. Most people are happy to earn a decent salary and make a good living. Stability, you know?"

I nodded. "And stability is necessary, absolutely. I'm anxious when I don't have it. I just feel like there is so much more to life. I spend my time digging into historical facts, learning about people and the lives they lived, the memories they created. And I want to be one of those people. I want to be one of the girls that had memories that someone else might find one day. What good is my life if I leave nothing behind to show that I existed at all?"

Dane looked surprised. "I had never thought about it that way, but the point of being alive, of existing, is to leave a legacy behind."

I nodded, so excited that he was getting the point of what I was saying.

"I mean, it's essentially what I'm doing too."

"That's just the thing," I said. "And being in New York, working myself to death, making someone else successful, just didn't do for me what it needed to. I couldn't find my footing. And what was worse, I didn't like the hustle and bustle, either. It was too busy, too cramped. No one stopped to smell the roses."

Dane chuckled. I knew he thought about the roses at the estate, and I smiled.

"I love the serenity of Pinewood," I concluded.

"You know," Dane said, leaning forward and placing his elbows on the table. "You are by far the most interesting woman I have ever met."

I blushed, surprised at the compliment. I had been called beautiful and sexy and hot so many times in my life, it was tiring. But to be called interesting? Men had never gone there with me.

"I am?" I asked, sounding like an idiot. I just didn't understand how he could think that.

"You are," Dane confirmed. "Interesting, and smart. You don't seem to want what the usual people want, and that makes you interesting. You're different, and I like that."

I couldn't help myself. I blushed again. But I had to admit, Dane wasn't quite mainstream, either. And even though I wouldn't say so to his face—I was far too shy—he was extremely interesting, too.

"So, you must be quite familiar with most of the people in town," Dane said. "After all, they would have made it their business to know exactly who you are and what you're doing."

I laughed. "I'm not on a first name basis with them, if that's what you mean, but I do know that they all know who I am and where I come from."

"Doesn't it bother you?" Dane asked.

I thought about it for a moment, but then I shook my head.

"I don't really have anything to hide. And I like it when people care about me, when they reach out because I matter. I guess it ties in with not feeling like I had any kind of identity in the city."

Dane nodded slowly, thinking about what I had said. He seemed to have a very different view of the city than I did, but I liked that he was open-minded enough to consider my point of view. That wasn't something that a lot of people were willing to do.

"I can't wait until I am on a first name basis with at least eighty percent of the population," I joked. "I think I have only a few more to go."

Dane laughed. "Just don't make friends with old man Weiser."

"Who's that?" I asked.

They nodded toward the bar area. "That's the guy. He hangs out at the bar from the moment it opens until they kick him out and he's full of piss and vinegar. Once you get him talking, he doesn't stop. And I can promise you it's not nearly as interesting as anything I have to say. Or you."

I laughed again. Dane was so open and so comfortable to speak to. I loved how light he made me feel.

Who would have known that a move to a small town would bring Prince Charming? It was the last thing I had come here for, and the last thing I had thought I would find. After all, if you wanted to get married, they always said you had to go to a big city. There was a larger pool to choose from.

But I didn't need a large pool if there was someone like Dane around. He was so funny, so comfortable to be around, and he seemed genuinely interested in me. It was a triple whammy.

Could it be possible that he could be someone I could get involved with? I had never set out to date, but the idea of having someone to share my life with was intriguing.

After dinner, we didn't eat desert at the restaurant. Instead, Dane told me about an ice cream shop that he used to get desert from as a child.

"It started as a pop-up shop that was only supposed to last two weeks," Dane said while we walked there. The evening air was crisp on my bare arms and it smelled like Pine after which the town was named. "It's been fifteen years and the shop is still doing well. And you'll find out why."

"The best ice cream in the county?" I guess.

"You don't know what that means until you taste it."

We reached the shop and ordered our ice creams. Dane ordered a cone, but I asked for a cup. And when I took a bite, I had to admit, he was right.

"Do I know how to pick 'em, or do I know how to pick 'em?" Dane asked, holding his arms wide as if he was challenging me.

I laughed, nodding. "You sure know how to pick 'em."

We continued walking, eating ice cream and talking.

"Tell me about being a police officer," I said. Dane stiffened next to me. "How did you get into it? Did you always know it was what you wanted to do?"

Dane nodded. "My family has always been very wealthy, but all I kept seeing was people who didn't give back to the community in a way that mattered. It's not that they were bad people, they did their share of charity work and donations and that, but I felt like there had to be more I could do. So, I decided to become a police officer. Everyone gets in trouble once in a while, and it's great when there is a hero to save you."

"I think it's very noble," I said.

"Do you? My family didn't quite agree. My grandad was very upset about it."

"And your grandmother?" I asked. I was suddenly worried that it had come across too obvious that I was asking about Claire, hoping that he would drop some kind of hint.

But then shook his head and continued talking. "No, she's a sweetheart. She has always supported everything I wanted to do. But I think that she understands what it's like to have to break the rules to get what you want. My Gran is a tough old lady."

I wanted to ask more about his grandmother, about the estate. But I didn't want him to think that I had gone out with him tonight to pry about his grandmother and whether or not she was the Claire Whiteside I was looking for. Because I wasn't here with Dane for that reason. I had met him because of it, but I had accepted a date with him because I was genuinely attracted to him.

And as the night progressed, I became more so.

Chapter 21

Amelia

By the time we returned to the restaurant, where Dane had parked his car, we had finished our ice cream. And this was it, the date was over. Strangely, I didn't want to go back home. I didn't want this to end—I still wanted to spend more time with Dane.

But if he felt the same about me, if he was as attracted to me as I was to him, I was sure that I would see more of him and we would still have time. There was no reason to rush anything.

This was another reason why I had never been able to live in New York. Everything there was so rushed, including relationships. The few men that had been interested had wanted to fast track it, so I had never felt comfortable.

I wanted to make a point of keeping things slow, this time. I like Dane, and I wanted to give whatever this was a chance.

"Shall we call it a night?" Dane asked.

I nodded, hiding my reluctance.

"Can I drive you home?" Dane asked. "Unless you would prefer me to drop you off at the shop again. I am not trying to find out where you live or anything."

I laughed. "I don't think you're a stalker. Thank you, driving me home would be great."

Dane grinned at me and I couldn't get over how handsome he was. The way he looked at me alone made me swoon. His eyes slid down to my lips, and I wanted him to kiss me.

But instead, he turned away from me and my heart sank a little.

MY SWEETHEART

Maybe he wasn't as attracted to me as I had hoped. Maybe he just wanted to be friends. And I guess that was something I would be able to do—anything to spend a little more time with him. But I would have liked more.

When we walked back to his car, he opened my door for me again and I reveled in how special that made me feel. When he was behind the wheel, he allowed me to direct him to my apartment.

"Thank you for a great night," I said, when we stopped in front of my apartment building. "I really enjoyed myself."

"So did I," Dane said. I hesitated, giving him a chance to lean over and kiss me in the car, but he didn't. So, I opened the door and climbed out. He opened his door and climbed out, too. He walked around his car and joined me on the curb.

I wondered what he was doing. He didn't have to walk me to my door, the building door was right here. But then he stepped forward, put his hand behind my neck, and kissed me.

It was so out of the blue, and I melted. And damn, he was such a good kisser. His tongue slipped into my mouth and I leaned against him a little, drawn into him, absorbed by the moment.

When he broke the kiss, I was lightheaded and out of breath. He grinned at me with that million-dollar smile and a hint of arrogance that suggested he knew exactly what he was doing to me.

And because of everything—the night being so perfect, his company being so comfortable, his interest in my life—I couldn't help myself. I just wanted to share everything with him. I wanted to show him what I had found and share my excitement with him.

"Can I show you something?" I asked. "It's an antique, so you can say no if you want to."

He nodded. "I'd love to see what you want to show me."

I turned and unlocked the door to the building, letting him follow me in. We walked up the stairs to the second floor where I shared a small entrance hallway with Mrs. Mills. I unlocked my door and pushed it open, about to let Dane follow me in, when I thought of something and stopped in my tracks. I turned to him and suddenly I felt embarrassed.

"I really do just want to show you something. It's not what you think—I don't do that on a first date."

Dane chuckled, amused. "I completely respect that. I didn't think you had any ulterior motives. I'm really just interested in what you want to share with me."

I felt silly at reacting the way the way I had, but I was also relieved. With men, I could never tell if they had other things in mind until I was too far down the line, and I didn't want to have to push Dane away because I hadn't told him early enough what my intentions were.

I switched on the lights as we walked into the apartment, and I saw Dane look around. My apartment was a good size for me, but compared to where Dane lived, it was nothing. It was a small two-bedroom place with an open plan kitchen and a little living room. But I loved it.

"This is a very nice place," Dane said.

"Compared to where you live?" I asked.

Dane laughed. "Trust me, that is not where I live. It's my grandmother's place and I would give an arm and a leg to live like that, but I live in an apartment not too far from here."

I was surprised. For some reason I had thought that Dane lived with his grandmother, that the estate and all the money that was obviously there belonged to him, too.

"I'll be right back," I said, walking to the second bedroom that I had turned into an office. I opened the drawer in the desk and retrieved the letter. I ran my fingers around the corners, feeling the smooth envelope again. This was something so special to me, I hoped that Dane would understand and revere it in the same way.

When I came back to the living room, Dane had made himself comfortable on the couch. But he stood again when I walked in.

"No, please sit down," I said. I sat down next to him. "Here, this is what I wanted to show you."

Dane took the envelope from me and opened it.

"It really old," I said.

"I'll be careful," Dane said, understanding completely what I was saying. And I watched him take the letter out of the envelope carefully, making an effort not to bend any corners or be reckless with it. I was impressed with his care.

I watched as he unfolded the letter and started reading. When he reached the end of the later, he spoke.

"Are you serious?" he asked.

"Is she your grandmother?" I asked. I couldn't hold out any more.

"My grandmother is Claire, and her maiden name was Whiteside. It was what she named the Guild after. But this—where did you get this?"

"It came to the shop at the bottom of a box that someone dropped off."

I couldn't contain myself. The fact that Claire was Dane's grandmother was almost too good to be true. And even though I had told myself that I wouldn't ruin the date by bringing up Dane's grandmother and who she had been, I was practically humming with excitement. I could find all my answers right here if I just asked. I could find out if she had found her Thomas.

"So?" I asked. "Did she find him?"

Dane frowned and read the letter again. "There is so much love and passion in these words. And so much despair."

It wasn't an answer, and I was dying to know. But I didn't push for him to tell me right away. I could tell that his grandmother's words were touching him in a different way than it had touched me. I tried to swallow my curiosity and wait for Dane to speak.

"Sometimes, I wonder where her mind is at. I wonder what she thinks about when she disappears from me. I'm starting to wonder if it might be this."

I had no idea what Dane was talking about. And I was dying of curiosity.

"Did she find him?" I asked again, carefully this time. I didn't want to push Dane. For some reason, he was emotional. Nostalgic."

He looked up at me, and his dark eyes were sad. "I don't think she did."

My heart sank. I felt disappointment washed over me like a wave. This was wrong. How was it possible that after all these years, she hadn't found the man she loved so much?

"What do you mean?" I asked.

"I don't think she found Thomas," he said again. "I have never heard of this man. My grandfather's name wasn't Thomas."

My ears started ringing. It wasn't even my own love story, but I had dreams of the perfect ending. I had thought about Claire Whiteside and her love so much, it was like a punch to the gut that she might not have found her happiness.

"How could this be?" I asked. "How could she not have ended up with her true love?"

He pulled up his shoulders. "Sometimes, happy endings don't exist. Sometimes, we fall in love and we don't marry. Sometimes, our soulmates slip through our fingers before we even know it. That's reality."

I hated his definition of reality, even though he was right. For some reason, it only irritated me. It upset me. I was really sad that Dane didn't know Thomas. I was sad that Claire might not have realized her dreams.

"I think I have to go," Dane said. He seemed like he was in a sad mood, too. What was happening here? I wasn't sure what he was thinking about, and I didn't want to ask. This seemed a lot closer to home to him than to me, and if it affected me this much, it was doing something worse to him. It was clear to see.

Then he carefully folded the letter and put it back in the envelope. He put envelope on the coffee table before he stood. He turned to me.

"Thank you for a great night together," said. "Could I call you sometime?"

I nodded. "I would like that."

Dane turned to the door. I felt like something was wrong, though.

"I'm sorry," I said to Dane.

He stopped at the door and turned around. "For what?"

"For the letter," I said. "I didn't mean to dampen the mood."

Bane shook his head. "No, don't be sorry. I'm glad you showed me. And it was really fun to spend time with you, to get to know your interests. I'd like to do it again sometime."

Even though he was in a bit of a sad mood, I believed his words were genuine. Dane didn't seem like the kind of man who would only say the right thing to get into my pants. After all, if that was really his intention, he would have charmed me since the moment we had walked through the door.

No, something else was bothering him. But he was being upfront and honest with me.

"I'll call you sometime next week, and we can maybe get together for lunch or a coffee date," Dane said.

I nodded. "I'd like that," I said.

"Have a good weekend, Amelia," Dane said, and he left my apartment. He didn't kiss me again and the strange sorrow that had come over him when he had read the letter stayed behind in the apartment after he closed the door.

I looked at the letter on the coffee table again. I wasn't sure what had happened with Dane, but I was sad for Claire and the man she had loved so much. I couldn't imagine what it must be like to be ripped away from the man you thought you were going to spend the rest of your life together with.

What had happened? How had they not ended up together?

Why did the story not have a happy ending?

Chapter 22

Claire

I wasn't showing. I was only a couple of weeks, and I could still wear the clothing I had worn until now. I didn't know how I would hide the pregnancy once my stomach became bigger, but that wasn't my worry right now.

It was more difficult to hide my morning sickness from my parents. Especially my father, who was out and about more often again now. My mother often still locked herself in her room, but my father tended to spend time in the formal sitting room or sit at breakfast with me.

I also struggled to keep my appetite constant. Some days, I was so nauseous I couldn't even think about food without throwing up. Then it was torture sitting at the breakfast table, forcing food down my throat for the sake of appearances. I would always run to my room afterward and throw up again, even though I knew that I had to eat well for the pregnancy.

Other days, I was so hungry I couldn't stop eating, and I had to sneak food out of the kitchen if I didn't want to be caught. I didn't want to have to explain myself.

But, I was managing. And all the while, I was thinking of ways that I would be able to live my life without my family if it came down to it. Because I wasn't going to be able to hide this baby forever. And I didn't know how long I would still have to wait for Thomas to return.

What if he only came back well after I had given birth? I had to consider that I might have to raise this baby alone for a while.

I didn't even consider the option that I might have to raise the baby alone for the rest of my life. I wasn't going to go there. I wasn't going to think about whether or not Thomas might die. I was going to firmly believe that he was alive on the battlefield, that he would do what was necessary and that he would come back for me. That was my truth, my reality. And I held onto it tightly, allowing it to be the beacon of hope that guided me through the darkness that the war afforded.

At breakfast one morning, almost three weeks later, my father made an announcement.

"I think that we have had enough sorrow in this household."

I looked up at him, unsure what he was talking about. I hadn't exactly paid attention to his conversation for most of the morning, and it was just me and him.

"Agatha!" he called for my mother. "Agatha, you must join us. I have an announcement to make."

It took a while for my mother to appear from her room, and when she did, she looked sickly. But my father didn't seem to notice, or care. Or maybe he was used to her looking this way by now.

"I have decided that it's time to have a dinner party."

My mother frowned and I looked at my father in disbelief.

"A dinner party?" I asked. "In the middle of the war?"

My father nodded. "I have said it before and I will say it again. We cannot stop living because of this war. There will be nothing of us left."

"But within reason, father," I said. "A dinner party seems extravagant, and unnecessary. What about the food it will require? And the people that will have to come here, how unsafe will it be for them?"

My father shook his head. "We need a little bit of light and life in this household. It has already been arranged. Tonight, we will host two other families and we will forget that the war is raging outside our windows."

"Tonight?" My mother asked, looking as shocked as I felt. "We have no time to prepare."

MY SWEETHEART

"Don't you worry about that, all the food will be delivered throughout the morning, and we only need to get the cook to put it together. And if the two of you work hard, we can have it all set up by sundown."

I shook my head, shocked. And my mother looked taken aback, too. My father was unpredictable at best, but sometimes I wondered if during the course of this war he had started losing his mind.

But there were no two ways about it. My father was insistent, and my mother and I had to jump to arrange things. The food arrived as he had told us, but by bit throughout the morning. Food we haven't been able to eat in months. Sugar and butter and cuts of meat. Fresh vegetables. Milk.

My stomach rolled when I looked at the food. I felt nauseous, but I didn't think I would throw up. Luckily. At least I would be able to help my mother without giving myself away.

"He has planned this for a while, hasn't he?" I asked my mother, when we stood in the kitchen, looking at the food that the cook was preparing.

My mother nodded. "He has. I was aware that he had something up his sleeve since the plans to go to the country had fallen through, but I didn't think it would be something like this. I have thought it would be something a little more permanent. But it would be best to indulge him. We all act differently in times of tragedy."

I nodded my head and didn't argue. I didn't agree with my mother, but arguing with her would be pointless. This piece was going to happen, and we had to make sure that everything was in order.

Of course, my father wasn't in the kitchen, helping us. It was beneath him to do work like this. Rather let the women work in the kitchen. He had been the one to organize this feast, but he was locked in his office now, doing who knows what.

By the time the sun was low on the horizon, I walked back to my room to get dressed for the evening. My father had told us that it was a semiformal event, and I had to put on something agreeable.

I went through my closet. I had a few dresses that looked good on my figure, but I felt bloated and uncomfortable. My pregnancy did not show just yet, but I was self-conscious.

In the end, I chose a dress that flared from my waist a little, hiding my lower stomach although there was nothing to see.

And when I emerged from the room, my father waited for me.

"You look wonderful, my darling girl," he said. "I think you will enjoy tonight very much."

My father was being strangely affectionate, and I wasn't sure why.

But there wasn't time to ask him. Because the first guests arrived, and my father put his business smile on his face, marching to the front door with me and my mother in tow.

The first couple was older than my parents, and both their sons had gone to war. They looked tired and rundown, as if they had spent months and months worrying. But they were polite, smiling when they needed to, and complimenting my mother on her home.

The second couple was more my parents age, and they had a son who wasn't at war. Apparently, he had asthma.

They made a point of telling us so, immediately, so that we would not dare believe that Reggie Peters was a deserter.

And immediately, I disliked the man. Yes, he was handsome. Tall, blonde, with broad shoulders and upright manner. But he was arrogant and full of himself. Pompous.

And he was American. As were his parents, although they didn't rub it in your face the way he did.

"I must say, it's grand of our troops to come help in an hour of need, eh?" he joked, when the discussion turned to the American soldiers. It rubbed me the wrong way and I bristled. I thought of Thomas, cold and hungry, possibly hurting out on the battlefield, and this man who dared laugh about it.

"It's a pity that so many ~~lies~~ lives have to be sacrificed," I said. "Even American ones, when war is so unnecessary."

"I disagree," Reggie said. "War is necessary. It is a part of natural selection. Dominance is in our nature and it is normal to fight for territory."

I was horrified. "What about all the lives that are being lost, the cities that are bombed, the families that are being torn apart."

"Nature can be cruel," Reggie said. He was nonchalant about what he was saying, and I couldn't believe that a man would have so little regard for human lives. I couldn't stand him. He was only saying that war was a necessary evil because he had not been deployed. If he had been out there, his own life on the line, perhaps he would be singing a different tune.

Before we sat down to dinner, my father came to me with a broad grin.

"What do you think of Reginald?" He asked me.

He was talking about Reggie. Reginald was too elite of a name to describe someone like him. Of course, I couldn't say that to my father.

"I think this dinner party is a little unnecessary, given the circumstances." It was about as rebellious as I dared to go while we were in front of people. My father would not hesitate to berate me in company, and I didn't want a scene. I already felt uncomfortable, nauseous.

"Let's eat," my father said, his disapproval clear on his face.

When we sat down at the table, I was purposely placed next to Reggie. And I hated it. In fact, the whole dinner felt like a courtship. I was put off by the very idea of being set up with someone like Reggie.

How could my father possibly think about marrying me off to someone during a time like this? How could he be thinking about business moves and dinner parties and matchmaking when people were dying out there?

I couldn't tell him that my heart belonged to Thomas, or that I was carrying his child, but it only made me more determined to dislike Reggie for everything he was. Because I had found someone who was so much better and so much purer than Reggie would ever be.

The rest of the dinner party was a drag. It was difficult to keep track of the conversation. I was exhausted and I found it hard to concentrate.

And every now and then, my father made jokes that put me and Reggie on the spot. When that happened, Reggie took over and pretended to be the person that would protect me, boisterous and frustrating. Everything that came out of his mouth was offensive.

As the night dragged on, I felt sick. The nausea was building, my exhaustion was taking over, and I wanted nothing more than to go to bed. But it would be rude to excuse myself unless I had a good reason.

Maybe, if I threw up all over Reggie, I would be excused.

I entertained the thought when my father called me to the side.

"How did you enjoy yourself tonight?" he asked. "Don't you find the Americans fascinating?"

I really didn't, but I nodded once. I didn't want to get into an argument. I was too tired.

"Next week, Reggie and his parents will be returning to the USA. They are going to go home."

I envied them. I wished that I could find Thomas and we could escape to the country we had been dreaming about since we had met.

"You are going with them," my father said.

I stared at him, blinking. "What?"

"It's not safe here, Claire. I don't want you in a country that could be bombed at any moment. And there is no future in a country like this, especially not if the Germans take over. It would be better for you to go with them. I've arranged it all."

"And I have no say in this?" I asked.

My father shook his head. "You're not thinking clearly at the moment. I know that you don't want to let go of the home you grew up in, but everything we knew before is in the past. It's time to look to the future now. Your future."

An ominous feeling sank onto me, and I had an idea I knew what he was saying.

"What am I going as?" I asked.

My father's eyes sparkled. He was excited. But my stomach turned and I knew that this was it, this was hell.

"As Reggie's fiancé."

Chapter 23

Thomas

I had gotten separated from my group. The one moment we had all been together, then a set of planes had come over us, dropping bombs on the buildings around us, and we had scattered.

I had run in a direction, following the other soldiers, but dust flew up with clumps of earth showering me, and then suddenly, a loud bang had shattered my hearing. My ears had rung for half a day, and I had laid in the dirt, waiting for the end to come.

But it didn't, and eventually, I had stood. Looking around me, I realized that I was completely alone. I shouldn't have stayed on the ground so long, shouldn't have gone down in the first place. But I was tired, my body was weak and I couldn't think clearly. I didn't know when I last had food or sleep, and I was dying of thirst.

All the soldiers were in the same state at this point. How anyone was going to stand up and fight was beyond me.

I headed in a direction because it was as good as any. I chose a point on the horizon and I started walking. I walked and I walked until my legs screamed at me to stop, my lungs burned as if I had been running. But it was better than nothing. It was better than lying down right there and curling up in a ball. Although that sounded just as good.

Suddenly, there was a troupe of German soldiers in front of me. They looked healthy and well rested. Again. How did this keep happening?

One of them looked in my direction and saw me. He turned a rifle on me and opened fire. Despite being as exhausted as I was, with no energy at all, I still found it in myself to run. I ran faster than I had thought I was capable, and I tripped over the roots of trees and shrubs in front of me. When I went down, it was into a ditch. I tried to stop my fall with my hands, and scraped my palms raw.

I heard a grunting sound when I scrambled up, and realized that I had almost landed on top of someone else. For a moment, I was terrified it was another German soldier. I would be dead for sure, then.

But it looked like one of ours. American, or British. It was difficult to tell he was so plastered with mud.

"Don't shoot," he whispered.

I shook my head and pressed my fingers to my lips. I pointed up toward the top of the dip and hoped that he understood. If we were quiet enough, lying in the mud and covered by dried leaves, maybe the soldiers wouldn't see us.

I didn't know how long it was that we lay in the leaves, waiting for the German soldiers to disappear. I didn't think it mattered. I needed to rest and my aching bones were relieved to be able to lie down for a while. I was terrified, but fear had become the soundtrack of my life. I was getting used to the taste of bile at the back of my throat, the sense of fear that hung around us, the feeling of my legs going numb or my brain shorting out when I thought it was the end.

How many times had I been here? And how many times would I still be forced to deal with something like this? Everyone I had known was either missing or dead.

There were nights where I woke up screaming, seeing Harry's busted face over and over again.

I was so damn thirsty. If I didn't find water soon, I would be screwed. All that my canteen held was dust.

And right there, in the ditch, somewhere at the bottom of Poland, I could feel myself giving up hope. This war was a lost cause.

When we had been recruited in the states, told that we were coming to Europe to help fight against the Germans, I had been excited to get involved. I had never believed that sitting on my hands was a way to get through life, and helping others in need had followed a close second to the proactive habits I had grown up with.

But despite coming here to help, the war was only getting worse. We were losing men, not gaining ground.

There was no way of knowing how long this would carry on. Sometimes, I believed that it would continue forever.

But what was the worst of all, what really made this entire thing as dark as night for me, no matter what time of day I found myself in, was that I hadn't heard from Claire. Not for weeks.

After that first letter I had received after being deployed out of Romford, I hadn't heard a single word from her again.

Of course, I should have considered that it was because I was all over the place. Sometimes I wasn't even sure of what country I was in. But the truth was, I was starting to doubt what we had shared. At first, it was all that had gotten me through. I had looked back at the time we had spent together, the promises we had made and I held onto it like a lifeline. But I didn't know if that was what Claire wanted anymore. I had walked into this war with so much hope, so much courage, and I had lost so much.

It would only make sense if I lost this, too.

If she heard me now, the woman she used to be to me, she would have scolded me for giving up so easily. She was as strong headed as anything, and it was part of what I loved about her. But the war had clawed away at everyone, and the person I was now wasn't the same man I used to be.

And what about her? Would she still be the same woman? I highly doubted it.

"Come on, we have to find water," the other soldier said, and I remembered that he was still here. The sun was very high in the sky and I wondered if I had drifted off and been dosing while we had been lying in the leaves. Judging by how confident the other soldier looked, the Germans must have been long gone.

I pushed myself up with difficulty. My muscles ached and my bones felt brittle. And I didn't see the point of carrying on.

"I think there's a watering hole nearby," the soldier said. "Get on your feet and follow me. My name is Ray."

"Thomas," I said, and shook the hand that was offered, even though I didn't care who he was. But I did as he said, I got up and followed him. And by some miracle, we found the waterhole.

I should have been more excited about it than I was. Finding water was finding life, after all, but I had given up so completely, that if I hadn't found water at all, I don't think I would have been too upset about it.

We drank water and we filled our canteens. And then we sat together next to the watering hole for a while. Neither of us seemed to care that we were out in the open.

"Where are you from?" Ray asked. He was British, the accent coming through clearly, now. It reminded me of Claire and I didn't like it.

"Montana," I said. Before, I would have mentioned London, because my heart had been there. But now, I was just thinking about home.

"We'll get you back there, yet, soldier," Ray said.

How did he do it? How was he still full of hope? How did he still believe that we would get out of here?

I thought about it for a minute, and then I shook my head.

"No, I don't think we will." With great difficulty, I stood.

"Where are you going?" Ray asked.

"Away from here," I said.

"Why? It would be better for us to stick together. We have a greater chance of surviving, then."

I shook my head again. I wasn't going to get attached to another person, make another friend that could die on my watch. I wasn't going to put myself in a situation where I would sacrifice myself for someone—because that was what I would do. I was done. I needed to be alone. If I lived, then it would be of my own accord. And if I died? Well, that would be that, then.

I was tired. My soul was exhausted. And I couldn't do this anymore. I wasn't going to stick around, I wasn't going to work the plan. I was going to get up and I was going to start walking.

And when I was tired of walking, I was going to stop. Because I just wanted this to be over. I couldn't do it anymore. I wouldn't. I had never felt this low in my life, like there was nothing left to live for. But today, I was sure that if I died, it wouldn't matter.

"If you run into Germans now, they're going to kill you," Ray shouted after me.

I didn't respond. I wasn't going to let him tell me what to do. I wasn't going to let him take responsibility for me, and if I died he would struggle with the same nightmares I had with Harry. I was going to become no burden to anyone, and make no one a burden of mine.

Every time we had been in a war, fighting against the Germans, it had felt like the sun had disappeared, crawling behind the crowd as if it didn't want to witness the horrors of this earth. But today, there wasn't a cloud in the sky and the sun beat down on my brow. It felt like it was draining me of the little life I had left. I was tired and dried out, despite having had water only a short while ago. Or how long had it been? I wasn't even sure anymore.

I just kept walking. At some point, the water in my canteen ran out. And even then, I just continued. I was out in the open, a man alone, like a sitting duck.

But I didn't care. If someone wanted to take me out, let them. If a German was going to shoot at me, well done. And if they would leave me alone, I would just keep walking until I either reached the end of this war, or until I died. That was all that was left for me. There was nothing to go home to, no one to find.

I was almost a hundred percent sure that Claire had given up on me. Because if I couldn't even believe in myself, how could I expect someone else to?

And as soon as I decided that there was nothing left to live for, I felt oddly free. I had no obligations, no responsibilities, nothing. All that mattered now was that fate would decide if it wanted me around a little longer.

Chapter 24

Amelia

After Dane left, I felt terrible. I felt like I had ruined a wonderful date night, and I felt like I had ruined his mood. I should have thought about what it could mean if I showed him the letter, but I had been so caught up in my own excitement that I hadn't thought that far.

And I had no way of reaching him. I didn't have his number and I didn't know where his apartment was. I couldn't very well drive to the estate and knock down the old lady's door to tell her that I wanted to apologize to Dane. But I desperately wanted him to know that I was sorry. I hadn't meant to make things more difficult. I'd never intended to be insensitive.

The way he had left my apartment left me feeling like I had screwed something good up. Because Dane really was something good. I hadn't met someone like him in my life before, and I didn't want things to go south even before anything started between us. I wanted to get to know him better, I wanted to spend more time with him.

Fat chance of that happening, now. I was the woman who had screwed everything up.

Oh well, I guess that that was that, then. I would see Dane around town, no doubt. Pinewood wasn't very big and there were only so many people I could run into before one of them would be Dane.

By then, I guess it would be too late. An apology that late would be pointless.

I stood and took the letter back to the office, tucking it into the top drawer where I had found it. When I had showed Arthur, after he had come back from his trip, he hadn't been nearly as excited about it as I had been.

"Letters are often dead ends," he had said. "I get excited about objects because they are driven by concrete facts. Letters are driven by abstract emotions and those never last."

I had been confused about his reaction then. Arthur was always so excited about things that were old, about finding out stories about people.

But I was starting to understand what he meant. Because human emotions were fickle and fleeting, weren't they? That letter had proved it. Not that I had known what had happened, but I was disappointed that the love story hadn't had a happy ending, and I barely knew anything about either of the people.

If I had found something like an engagement ring in the envelope, would it have made a difference? Because that was solid, concrete with information attached to it, wasn't it?

I wasn't sure if I agreed with Arthur about letters having so little meaning. This letter had so much meaning to me.

Either way, it didn't matter now. The story hadn't had a happy ending, and Dane was upset with me, now. Or maybe not upset with me, but I was the reason he was upset.

I was about to go to my bedroom and get ready for bed when a knock sounded on my door. I walked to the front door and opened it.

Dane stood in front of me.

"You're back," I said.

Dane nodded. "I didn't want to seem rude that I left the way I did. I think I was a little caught up in my emotions."

"I'm so glad you came back. I was feeling guilty for dropping a bomb on you."

Dane shook his head, stepping into the apartment. "I have to be honest with you, it was a lot to swallow. My Gran has been struggling for quite some time, and I'm starting to understand why. But it wasn't a bomb that you dropped on me. I actually think that this might be exactly what my Gran needs."

I frowned. "What do you mean?"

"I think that she's been thinking about this man. Thomas. I have been asking her about my grandad, if she misses him. But she only shuts down on me when I do. And the other day, she was staring into the distance and she told me that she thought I was someone else. I think that she is starting to slip into her mind, and I think that is where this man lives. I think that if we give her the letter, it might cheer her up a little."

I was surprised. Of all the things I had expected to happen when I finally managed to apologize to Dane, this wasn't one of them.

"I would love for her to have the letter, and to go back to the day she wrote it."

"You should give it to her," Dane said. "I think it will mean a lot to her."

I thought about it for a minute. "How about we give her the letter together?" I asked.

Dane smiled at me. "I like the sound of that."

It was a dashing smile, and I smiled back at him. And suddenly, something between us shifted. I didn't know what it was, why the atmosphere was suddenly so thick and heavy. But I was aware of Dane and the fact that he was in my apartment. That he was standing close to me and that his eyes were boring into mine.

And the moment I thought it, his eyes slid down to my lips. His chest rose and fell with his breathing, and I couldn't help but stare at his lips, too.

Then stepping forward, he grabbed my head between his hands and kissed me.

The kiss was urgent, serious. I felt the hunger, the desire that he conveyed. It burned on my skin, the heat dancing between us, and I needed to be with him. I didn't know what it was that I felt.

I had never been so drawn to someone, or felt so connected in such a short time. It felt like being with Dane was right. More right than anything I had felt before.

And it wasn't because of lust, either. That was there, absolutely. But if felt like I had known these lips for a thousand lifetimes.

Dane tugged at my shirt, pulling it up so that his palms were on my bare skin. And even though is hands were calloused, strong, rough hands. But he touched me gently, like I was delicate. He pressed the length of his body against mine and I could feel his need for me. It mirrored my own.

I started unbuttoning his shirt, running my fingers through his chest hair when his shirt fell open and he shrugged out of it, shaking his hands when the cuffs got stuck over his knuckles. I helped him get rid of it, dropping the shirt on the floor.

Dane pushed me toward the couch, but I shook my head. I wanted to go to my room. I wanted to take the time to explore him.

When I led him to my bedroom, I could feel his eyes burning on my skin and he ran his hands down my arms. He spun me around in the room and pulled my blouse over my head before he kissed me again. His hands found my breasts and he massaged them, kneading them until I gasped into his mouth. My body was made of heat and I was so wet and ready for him. I wanted him to take me.

He reached behind my back and unclasped my bra with one hand, his other hand moving down to my pants and undoing them, too. He knew what he was doing. I didn't think about why, or what he'd done in his past life.

That didn't matter. What mattered was what we were doing, now.

Dane pushed me back onto the bed and he pulled my shoes off, and then my pants, taking my panties along with them so that I was naked.

I lay in the puddle of need in front of him, looking up at him, and his eyes slid over my body with adoration and wonder.

"You are incredible," he said.

I blushed.

"You're not just interesting, you're beautiful, too. And hot as hell."

Many men had told me that, for the sake of getting me in bed. But when Dane said it, I felt it. I believed it.

"You're only semi-naked," I said.

Dane grinned and undid his buckle. He pulled down his pants and kicked them off, naked now, too. He was so unapologetic about it. He was confident and proud and being naked with him seemed right.

He crawled on the bed and kissed me, lowering his body on top of me so that we were skin-on-skin, but he didn't crush me. Nothing was between us and I shivered at the intimacy.

Dane kissed me again, and while he did, he ran his hands over my body, tracing my curves with his fingertips. He pushed his hand between my legs and pushed his fingers into my sex. And I moaned.

Everything he did was without ceremony. It was straightforward and to the point. But at the same time, he did it with care so that I didn't once feel that it was just about sex. And the way he looked at me while he did it made me feel like there had been no other before me.

How was this possible? How had I met him only a few days ago, yet now felt like the most natural thing in the world was for our bodies to collide? It was as if we had been searching for each other, without knowing it, and now that we were finally together, it was a sigh of contentment, as if my bones could finally rest because my soul sighed 'there you are.'

Dane shifted on top of me and he positioned himself at my entrance. I held my breath and when he pushed into me, splitting me wide, it wasn't only my core that he penetrated, but my soul.

He started moving inside me. His dick was impressive and I had to get used to his size, but he moved inside me the same way he touched me. As if he was more than aware of his size and his strength and he knew exactly how much I could handle and what he had to do to hold back.

Slowly, he started moving faster and faster. He hit all the right spots, he pushed all the right buttons and the heat built inside of me, rising, filling me up until I was going to spill over.

And then I did, coming undone at the seams, letting go with a cry. My body clamped down around his and he grunted. But I wasn't aware of the sexual energy that rode me as waves of pleasure rolled over me. I was aware of Dane and how close he was to me.

When I came down from my sexual bliss, he started fucking me again. He pumped into me harder and faster, his hips bucking against mine and his rhythm became almost primal. He was pushing for his own release now. I curled and squirmed under him, riding it out with him, going as far as he would push me.

He groaned on top me, his body tense until I felt him kick and jerk inside of me as he released. He filled me up even more than he had until now. But his face was in my neck, his lips against my skin and I didn't only feel his orgasm, but I felt the connection with his lips against my shoulder, my neck, my jaw.

Finally, he stopped trembling on top of me and we both relaxed. His body collapsed on top of me. He was still buried inside of me, but we were connected in a way I hadn't been before and it was bliss.

Eventually, he rolled off and slipped out of me. And we were no longer merged to each other. But whatever bond we had forged now, whatever this strange connection was between us, it stretched out like taffy when he rolled away and even though we were no longer touching, we were by no means detached from each other.

Chapter 25

Dane

I woke up in Amelia's bed the next morning, and being here was the best place to be in the world. It felt right.

For the first time in a long time, the anxiety that haunted me was gone. It didn't feel like a monster inside me, ready to rear its ugly head in the form of a panic attack. For the first time since the shooting, I was at ease.

I had no idea what had happened between us last night. She had made it so clear that she wasn't inviting me up for sex, but in the end, we had slept together. Although, that didn't feel like what it was. Somehow, it had felt like we had connected on a different level.

She was still asleep when I opened my eyes and I watched her sleeping for a moment, thinking about how beautiful she was. From the moment I had met her, I knew there was something different about this girl.

And even now, after we had slept together, I was filled with the burning desire to get to know her better, to have her in my life somehow. It had happened the very first moment I had seen her.

And ever since, I hadn't been able to get her off my mind.

She rolled over and her eyes fluttered open. When she saw me, a smile spread over her face and she covered her mouth with the sheets.

"Morning," she said.

"Hello," I said with a smile.

"You stayed."

"I didn't want to leave."

MY SWEETHEART

We looked at each other for a moment, something passing between us that I was yet to understand. Every now and then when I was with her, I felt this strange sensation and I had no idea what it meant. All I knew was that I wanted more of it.

"How are we going to do today?" Amelia asked.

We had decided to give my gran her letter together. I wanted Amelia to see what my gran would think when she saw it. And I was dying of curiosity about Thomas, a man who had clearly had my gran's heart, but a man she had never mentioned, ever.

"I think I need to get to my apartment and change into fresh clothes, maybe have a shower. And then we can meet up for a cup of coffee before we head over there?"

Amelia nodded. "That sounds like a good idea. I want to shower and freshen up, too."

I kissed her on the forehead and got out of bed. I searched for my clothes that we had scattered through the house. While I got dressed, I was aware of Amelia's eyes on me. When I looked at her and caught her staring, she blushed

"I don't know what this is," she said. She was talking about us.

"Me neither. But we can figure it out. I'd really like to."

"Yeah. Me too. But first things, first."

I nodded.

I left her house, and after I showered, shaved, and changed into fresh clothes, I met Amelia had the coffee shop next to her work. Apparently, Amelia and Beth, the barista, were friends. When we ordered our coffees, she waggled her eyebrows at Amelia, who blushed.

We found a small table in the corner and sat down.

"I can't tell you how I exited I am about this," I said.

Amelia looked surprised. "Really? I thought this wasn't your thing."

"Antiques aren't really my thing. But this—this is personal. And if they all have stories like this, I'm starting to understand why you might be so serious about it."

Amelia offered me the broadest smile and it was beautiful. Everything about her was beautiful.

"I'm really excited, too," she admitted. "I've been dreaming about what happened to them, what their story is, since I found this letter. And to think that I might get an answer is amazing. Usually, I don't get the full story. The owners are often dead or long gone, or the pieces were passed on to other people so many times that no one knows the full story anymore. So this is new for me."

I reached across the table and squeezed her hand.

"What are the odds of this happening? Of us meeting, and you being the grandson of the woman who wrote this letter?"

I laughed. "Amelia, you drove onto my grans property like you were a tourist. It wasn't coincidence that we ran into each other, you were there, looking for trouble. And you found it."

"I did," she said with a grin. "And boy, did I ever find it."

We laughed and finished our coffee before we headed out. I drove us to my gran's house in my car. On the way, I could tell Amelia was nervous. And I understood why. But me? I was just excited.

This was exactly what my grandmother needed. I was sure that it was the one thing that would cheer her up when she hadn't been in a good space. I was excited to bring her something that would turn things around for her.

"Do you think she'll remember it?" I asked, suddenly wondering if it would do anything at all. What if I was betting on something that wouldn't even work?

"Of course she will. A woman will never forget her first love."

When we arrived at the estate, I parked where I usually did and Amelia and I walked to the house. I saw her looking around, admiring the house and the gardens. I wondered what went through her mound.

What she trying to imagine what my Gran's life might have been like between when she had written the letter, and now? Because I found that I was starting to think that way. When I had met Amelia, I had told her that antiques hadn't been an interest at all. But now that we were on this little mission, finding out things about the past, I was starting to see the appeal.

It was exciting.

I wondered if my Gran still thought about Thomas. I wondered if this was what she was thinking about when she slipped away from me, when her eyes glazed over and it was like she was in a different world. I'd always been aware that my Gran had a life, long before I had come onto the picture. She was much older than I was, and it was normal. But when you were a child, you tended to see only your own little world. And it was only now that I was starting to look further than that. Not just in terms of my Gran's life, but in terms of the world in general, thanks to Amelia.

We stopped outside the door that led to the living room. It was a smaller room, separate from the main living room, and my Gran called it a parlor, like they used to have in the old days.

I knew that she would be in there, now. It was the right time of day, and it was the perfect place for Amelia to meet her.

"I'm nervous now," Amelia said. "I mean, more nervous than before."

I took Amelia's hands in mine and squeezed them.

"She's going to love you, first of all. You're such an exciting person, you're so great. And she's going to be so happy to get the letter, too. It's going to be wonderful to see her reminisce, to hear the stories. Don't worry about a thing, this is going to be fun."

Amelia nodded, taking a deep breath and letting it out slowly.

I knocked on the parlor door and heard my Gran call from the other side. I opened it and asked Amelia to wait outside.

"Good morning, Nanna," I said, walking to my Gran where she sat in her favorite spot in the sun, knitting.

"Morning, Dane," she said with a smile. "You look well today."

I nodded and kneeled before my Gran. "I have someone here who wants to meet you. She found something that belongs to you. Is it all right with you if I show her in?"

"What did she find?" My gran asked.

"I would like for her to show you herself."

My Gran put her knitting away and touched her hair, making sure that she looked fine. But she would always look beautiful, regal even, to me.

"You can show her in," my Gran said.

I walked back to the door and told Amelia that she could join us. Amelia swallowed hard and stepped into the room.

"Good morning, Mrs. Peters," Amelia said. "My name is Amelia and I work at the antique shop in town. I found something that I believe belongs to you."

"Yes, Dane tells me that you have something that might be of interest to me. The antique shop, you said? I thought perhaps it had something to do with my roses."

"Oh, no. Your roses are beautiful, though. As is your home. But this, I believe, is a little more personal."

Gran frowned and nodded at Amelia, curious about what it was. Amelia opened her bag and took out the letter that she had carefully put inside *it* that morning. She handed it to my Gran and we both watched her with bated breath, waiting for a response.

I watched my Gran turn the letter over and over in her hands, her eyes studying the handwriting, her face carefully blank, so that neither of us would know what she was feeling. Then, she looked up at Amelia.

"It's very sweet of you to bring this to me. But tell me about you. I haven't seen you before, do you live in town?"

I was taken aback a little about how my gran was acting. She was making small talk with Amelia. Was she postponing her reaction? Or did she not recognize the letter at all? I didn't understand why she was acting this way.

"Are you not curious about the letter?" I asked. Because I was dying of curiosity.

My gran looked at me. "It's rude not to get to know our guests, first," she said.

And maybe, with the way Gran had grown up, it was rude. So, I fetched Amelia a chair and I pulled one closer for me, too. We both sat down and my Gran called one of the servants to make us tea. If we were going to sit here all day, making small talk before we got to the letter, then I guess that was what we were going to do. Because I knew that Amelia wasn't going to leave here without finding out what my gran thought of the letter and what had happened to Thomas. And I wasn't going to do that, either. I was far too involved, now.

Besides, the way that Amelia was intrigued by this love story, the way that she became excited about the ending, and the way that Gran was completely shut off about it, had me more than curious.

Besides, when I had been with Amelia last night, I had felt something that I had never felt with a woman before. And now that we were exploring this age old love story, I was more interested, because I felt that maybe, somehow, this love could possibly be true.

Until now I had been pessimistic about love—I had been sure it was just a chemical reaction and lust. But things were different, here, weren't they? Everything had changed for me the moment I met Amelia.

And I hoped that everything would change for Gran, too. Amelia seemed to do that for people.

Chapter 26

Dane

Claire was everything I imagined she would be. She was upright and elegant, poised even in her old age. This was like a fairytale come true. And even though I hadn't imagined that Claire was actually British, the moment she had spoken and I heard her accent, I had known it was right. I could hear the letter in her voice now, the way she carefully pronounced the words in such a prim way.

Speaking to her was so interesting. She had taken the letter from me, but she was still insistent on finding out who I was. And it was such a pleasure. Whatever Dane had that drew me to him so much, it had clearly come from his grandmother. Claire was the perfect hostess and conversationalist, and I could imagine that she was a wonderful grandmother.

"I just wanted to follow my passion," I said, telling her about the reason I had moved to Pinewood. Everyone seemed to think that it was such a strange thing to leave the city behind, but Claire nodded when I said it.

"Without passion, all your efforts are for naught. It's important that you follow your heart, or you will end up somewhere you never wanted to be."

I nodded. She was so right. But I was brimming with excitement.

How long had it been since I had found the letter? It hadn't been that long ago, but somehow, it felt like years. It felt like I was finally going to discover the ending to my story. I was going to find out what had happened to Thomas, and why he wasn't here. Why Claire hadn't married him.

Why was she taking so long to get around to the letter? Did she know what it was? Did she know what it could mean?

I wondered if maybe she had forgotten, if the letter was just another envelope in her lap and she could talk to us with such a calm face because she didn't know what was at stake here.

But Claire didn't look like the type of woman who was senile, or dumb. I was sure that she knew exactly what this was.

And finally, Claire looked down at the letter in her lap.

"So, you have brought this back to me," she said. And when she said 'back' I knew that she knew exactly what it was.

She picked up the letter again, running her fingers along the edges. She became emotional, and I watched as her eyes filled with tears. When she looked at the letter, it was almost as if we weren't in the room with her anymore. Somehow, she was transported back in time.

"Nanna?" Dane asked.

As if her name had snapped her back to reality, she looked up at Dane. The emotion drained away from her face. She nodded and handed the letter back to me.

I frowned. "Don't you want to open it?"

Claire shook her head. "There is absolutely no reason for me to open it. I don't need to be told what it says. Besides, this is a reminder of a life long gone. In fact, a life I never had."

"Read it, Nanna," Dane urged.

Claire was suddenly angry. "How can you expect that of me? How can you walk in here and tell me that I should open a letter that reminds me of a time that I have been trying my entire life to forget? Did you ever consider that this might be painful to me? That this letter is something I never want to see in my life again?"

Dane search for words and I could see how he struggled to find them. I was quite shaken as well. Of all the reactions I had expected, this wasn't one of them.

"I am so sorry," I said, jumping in to find the words when Dane couldn't. "I thought it would help, that it would be something you would want to see. It's so special, after all."

Claire pursed her lips for a moment. "Special is a very relative term. Once upon a time, maybe this letter meant something to me. But now? It's just a reminder of a life that was ripped away from me after it had been dangled before me like a carrot. I'd had dreams, wishes, and hopes, but they had all been ripped away from me, shattered like London had been in the Blitz. The war is a time of my life that I never want to think about again, and I don't want to remember anyone that was a part of it, either."

She took a deep breath and let it out with a tremble, turning her face to the window.

"Nanna," Dane said, in a soft voice, reaching for her hand. Claire let him take it. "Don't you want to talk about it? It's clearly something very serious."

"What's there to talk about? Thomas? That's why you're here, isn't it? You want to know about him."

Dane and I both nodded. Because that was the truth, we wanted to know what had happened to him. We wanted to know where he was.

"I never heard from him again," Claire said, and my heart sank to my shoes. "And I don't care, either. I moved on. I had a full life, I was safe, and my children were safe. If I hadn't been able to escape London, I would have died just as my parents did."

That last sentence was gut wrenching. To have lost family during the war? I couldn't imagine how painful it must have been.

"I hope with all my heart that Thomas was lucky enough to survive the war and go home to his ranch, and that he was able to move on, too.

He deserved it. But the life that I lived, the life that I was offered, was enough to keep me happy. And I never looked back."

I glanced at Dane. I wasn't sure about her last statement, about not looking back. Dane looked unsure about which way to go with this. I had to admit that Claire's outburst was a little different than I had expected, too. But she looked like she was calming down, and maybe she would still speak about it. Dane looked hopeful.

"May I ask you a question?" I asked.

Claire turned her eyes to me, and for a moment I could see how beautiful she must once have been. In her younger years, Claire Whiteside must have been the most beautiful girl in the world. It wasn't only in the way she carried herself, or the way she expressed herself, but there was something in the lines on her face that suggested she had been stunning. Was that what Thomas had seen when he had looked at her? I wished I could see a photo of her when she was young, so that I could try to put the picture in my mind.

"Ask," Claire said.

"Didn't you love him?"

It was as if I had asked the wrong question, as if I had burst the wrong dam. Immediately, Claire was furious. She glared at me with eyes that shot fire, and the frail old lady in front of me turned into a dragon.

"I was a child. Foolish. What do you know about love when you are seventeen? I regret sneaking out of my house that night and setting foot in that blasted bar. Thomas was the worst thing that ever happened to me."

Her words were spoken with so much venom, so much hatred, I couldn't imagine that this lady was the same person who had written that love letter, where every word dripped with emotion.

"I think we should go," Dane said to me. And I agreed. I wanted to get out of here. I stood as well.

"Thank you for having me, Mrs. Peters. I am so very sorry to have upset you."

Claire didn't answer me. She only turned her head back to the window, and pretended like I wasn't there. Dane and I left the parlor in a hurry.

As soon as we were outside, I let out a breath I hadn't known I'd been holding.

"I am so sorry," I said to Dane. "I had no idea it was going to go this badly. I thought it would be a good idea to bring the letter to her, to find her and to find out about their love story."

"Don't be sorry, I thought the same thing. I have no idea what happened in there. My gran has never spoken about her past and she refused to speak about the war. In all my life, I've never heard any stories about the war from her mouth. I didn't think that it would go like that, either. If anyone is to blame, it's me. I should have known better."

I covered my face with my hands and shook my head. I had been wanting to meet Claire Whiteside, but I regretted it, now. Not because of how she had reacted toward me, but because of the horrible memories I had obviously brought back to her. I felt terrible about disturbing the peace of a woman who clearly just wanted to forget.

In all my time looking at historical facts, looking at antique objects and finding the stories behind them, I had never found one that had such a tragic ending. And the worst was, I still had no idea what had happened. I didn't know what had happened to Thomas, or why Thomas and Clare had never ended up together. All that I knew was that I had really upset an old lady and brought up history that should have been left buried. I should have kept my nose in my own business.

"Really, don't beat yourself up about this," Dane said. But he looked worried and I knew that he was just as unsure about his gran's response as I was. And he had already been worried about her, about how she was slipping away from him. What if I had fast tracked that?

"Will you take me home?" I asked.

Dane nodded. "Do you want me to stay with you?"

I shook my head. "I think I just need to be alone for a while, and you'll want to check on her in a bit."

Dane didn't argue with me the way I thought he would. But maybe he understood. Maybe he realized exactly how I was feeling, because Dane seemed to understand parts of me that no one else had understood before. But I wasn't going to dig into exactly what I felt for Dane right now. I wanted to go home, I wanted to lick my wounds in peace. I wanted to forget.

All my life I had believed in soulmates, love at first sight, and happily ever-after's. I had believed that the fairytales were true, that the loving movies could exist, and that everyone could find if they just looked for it. It wasn't that I didn't believe in it anymore. The love that I had felt when I had read Claire's letter had been there.

But I also wasn't quite sure that happily ever after was a given anymore. I hadn't found mine. And clearly, Claire hadn't found hers. And what did that say about the rest of us? I was suddenly so confused about the concept of love. And I knew it was ridiculous, I shouldn't have let that affect my judgement at all. But still, seeing an old woman bounce between love and hatred like that, had really gotten to me.

"Are you ready?" Dane asked, after he had opened the door for me and walked around to the driver's side.

I nodded. I was ready to go home and try to put this behind me.

Chapter 27

Claire

America wasn't anything like I had imagined it. I had always seen it as a country of opportunity, a sort of safe haven for the lost and the broken. It was how they had depicted it for long, wasn't it?

But when we arrived, I found that life was like anywhere else in the world. Yes, there was far more space than in London, where I had spent most of my life, aside from vacationing in the country.

The houses were large, the land had so much more potential and everything seemed more relaxed. But I quickly realized that there were rules and regulations as there had been at home, there were families of money and class and families without, and the social hierarchy was something I understood.

And even though Reggie was a pompous man, boisterous on a good day and egotistical, he wasn't an awful person.

And his parents were simple people, despite the money they had acquired through the right investments at the right time. I found that they were good people, beneath the façade of too-good that they liked to carry around with them.

When my father had told me that I would travel to the United States with Reggie and his family, I had been heartbroken. I had planned to run away. I had shouted at my father and had cursed my entire lineage. I had said awful things to my parents that I was sure I would regret for the rest of my life, even when I had apologized a thousand times.

But one night, I had woken up after midnight with terrible sweats. I had been so nauseous I had spent the night with my head in a toilet bowl. And when I had finally been able to come up for air, the sound of war had been in the distance. Gun fire, and the earth had trembled lightly with the drop of bombs.

And not for the first time, I had feared for my life. But this time, I had also feared for the life of my child.

And I hadn't heard from Thomas. I still had no idea where he was. Or if he was alive. I had no idea if he was coming back. I was terrified that I would have to raise this child alone, disowned from my family with no money of my own, and no future as a woman who had been left by a man with a child, but not a ring.

And suddenly, the idea of traveling to the U.S. with Reggie had sounded like salvation. My child would grow up well-loved, in a home that he or she deserved. My parents would not disown me, and I would be looked after.

And the war? It would be so far behind me, I would be able to breathe easier again.

Thomas was the love of my life. I had given him my heart. But he wasn't here, at my side, and he couldn't take care of me, and our baby. I worried he never would be.

So, I had gone to my father and told him that I would go to the States with the Peters family. That I would be Reggie's wife.

And here I was.

"You look beautiful, darling," Mrs. Peters said, when I turned around in my white dress. I smiled at her. I wasn't beaming, I felt far too heavy for that. But I wasn't unhappy. Reggie was a good man and his intentions were not bad.

"Thank you for everything," I said.

"No, dear. Don't thank us. We're family, now."

The word left a hollow feeling inside of me, but I smiled and nodded, then together, we walked to the car that would take me to the church where I was to become Mrs. Reggie Peters.

The wedding was extravagant. It had been announced in all the papers and the guest list had five hundred people on it. That was for the wedding alone, the reception was even bigger. Newspapers were going to cover the event. I had five bridesmaids, all girls I didn't know. In fact, I didn't know any of the people at the wedding.

None of my friends or family had been able to attend. They were stuck in a war-stricken Europe.

When I stood on the steps, Mr. Peters came out of the church and smiled at me. He was going to give me way.

"You look perfect, dahlin' girl," he said, in his thick accent. I smiled and thanked him. He offered me his arm, and I took it. The doors open, the music started, and I took the first steps of the rest of my life.

When we walked down the aisle, I was a storm of emotion. The organ music was loud in my ears and it felt like it tugged at my insides. I was giving up everything I thought I wanted, at one time. I was turning my back on Thomas and our promises, giving up on our dreams.

My parents were here, my dad wasn't the one to give me way. And the spot where my mom should have stood with tears in her eyes was occupied by an aunt of Reggie's that I didn't even know.

My friends didn't know I was here, and I hadn't had a chance to say goodbye. And everything I had known as a child was gone. Not only because I had left, but because the war had ripped everything I knew and loved away from me.

So now, as I walked to the front of the church where Reggie was waiting for me, I felt as though I was a shell of the woman I once wanted to be. I felt like I was someone I didn't recognize. But war changed people. And so did love.

MY SWEETHEART

When I looked at Reggie, he was beaming at me. His smile was genuine and his eyes were warm, and with the way he looked at me, we could have been the only two people in the room.

Thomas had looked at me like that, once. But there had always been so much pain along with it. The separation, the war, the limited time together. I would be able to see Reggie every day of my life. He wouldn't leave me, he wouldn't go away to war and never return.

And we would be taken care of. Both me and my child. And we would be alright. We would be safe.

I had thought that getting married to Reggie would be dreadful. I had thought I was signing my life away.

But as I walked toward him, one step after the other, to the beat of the wedding march, I started feeling different. I started feeling better.

The heaviness of the war fell away. The constant worrying for my own life, for that of my child, and for Thomas's, stopped. And worry about money, or being disowned, and not having the approval of my parents for the rest of my life.

These were all worries I had carried with me, and the load had been so very heavy, I hadn't realized who I had become under the burden. But now as I walked to the front of the church, I felt as though I was changing. I was becoming lighter again. I was allowed to be the woman I wanted to be.

I didn't love Reggie. But I could learn to. I wasn't happy, but I could become so. This was safe, for me and the baby. This made sense.

When I reached Reggie and his father put my hand in his, I smiled at him. He wasn't my Prince Charming, my handsome knight on a valiant steed. But without trying to be, Reggie Peters would be my salvation.

And sometimes, all a girl needed was to be saved.

Once the ceremony was over, we stood on the steps of the church, waiting for all the newspapers to snap the photos. Reggie held my hand and I put on my most charming smile.

I would not show on the photos in the paper. No one would know I was pregnant. And in a few weeks, once the marriage had been consummated and Reggie and I were in a routine of sorts, I would tell him I was pregnant.

No one would know the difference. No one would know that he wasn't the father. No one but me.

I felt a little guilty about being so dishonest. But it was a lie I needed to tell for the sake of my safety and for that of my child. And I had realized a short while ago that no despite loving Thomas, love wasn't always enough. And I loved the child within me more than anything in the world. I would do whatever it took to look after him or her.

The last of the cameras flashed and in that flash, I saw Thomas's face. I dwelled on it for two moments, and then I put it out of my mind forever.

Thomas was in my past. He was a choice I had made, a promise I had broken. And a piece of me would always be cracked when I thought of him. But Reggie was my future. A new life awaited me here, a life where I would be safe. I had no choice but to do what I had done.

This is what was best for me, and what was best for the baby.

This was where my future would lie. I had still made it to the States. Not quite to Montana, but close enough. And I could still think of new dreams, if I tried hard enough.

THE END

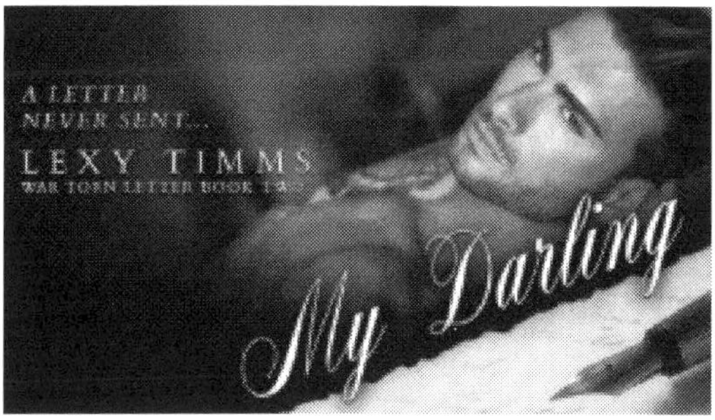
A LETTER
NEVER SENT...
LEXY TIMMS
My Darling

My Darling Blurb

Learn from yesterday, live for today, hope for tomorrow. The important this is not to stop questioning.
Albert Einstein

War Torn Letter Series

My Sweetheart - Book 1
My Darling - Book 2
My Beloved – Book 3

Find Lexy Timms:

LEXY TIMMS NEWSLETTER:
http://eepurl.com/9i0vD
Lexy Timms Facebook Page:
https://www.facebook.com/SavingForever
Lexy Timms Website:
http://www.lexytimms.com

Want

FREE READS?

Sign up for Lexy Timms' newsletter
And she'll send you updates on new releases,
ARC copies of books and a whole lotta fun!

Sign up for news and updates!
http://eepurl.com/9i0vD

More by Lexy Timms:

FROM BEST SELLING AUTHOR, Lexy Timms, comes a billionaire romance that'll make you swoon and fall in love all over again.

Jamie Connors has given up on men. Despite being smart, pretty, and just slightly overweight, she's a magnet for the kind of guys that don't stay around.

Her sister's wedding is at the foreground of the family's attention. Jamie would be fine with it if her sister wasn't pressuring her to lose weight so she'll fit in the maid of honor dress, her mother would get off her case and her ex-boyfriend wasn't about to become her brother-in-law.

Determined to step out on her own, she accepts a PA position from billionaire Alex Reid. The job includes an apartment on his property and gets her out of living in her parents' basement.

Jamie must balance her life and somehow figure out how to manage her billionaire boss, without falling in love with him.

** The Boss is book 1 in the Managing the Bosses series. All your questions won't be answered in the first book. It may end on a cliff hanger.

For mature audiences only. There are adult situations, but this is a love story, NOT erotica.

FRAGILE TOUCH

"HIS BODY IS PERFECT. He's got this face that isn't just heart-melting but actually kind of exotic..."

Lillian Warren's life is just how she's designed it. She has a high-paying job working with celebrities and the elite, teaching them how to better organize their lives. She's on her own, the days quiet, but she likes it that way. Especially since she's still figuring out how to live with her recent diagnosis of Crohn's disease. Her cats keep her company, and she's not the least bit lonely.

Fun-loving personal trainer, Cayden, thinks his neighbor is a killjoy. He's only seen her a few times, and the woman looks like she needs a drink or three. He knows how to party and decides to invite her to over—if he can find her. What better way to impress her than take care of her overgrown yard? She proceeds to thank him by throwing up in his painstakingly-trimmed-to-perfection bushes.

Something about the fragile, mysterious woman captivates him.

Something about this rough-on-the-outside bear of a man attracts Lily, despite her heart warning her to tread carefully.

Faking It Description:

HE GROANED. THIS WAS torture. Being trapped in a room with a beautiful woman was just about every man's fantasy, but he had to remember that this was just pretend.

Allyson Smith has crushed on her boss for years, but never dared to make a move. When she finds herself without a date to her brother's upcoming wedding, Allyson tells her family one innocent white lie: that she's been dating her boss. Unfortunately, her boss discovers her lie, and insists on posing as her boyfriend to escort her to the wedding.

Playboy billionaire Dane Prescott always has a new heiress on his arm, but he can't get his assistant Allyson out of his head. He's fought his attraction to her, until he gets caught up in her scheme of a fake relationship.

One passionate weekend with the boss has Allyson Smith questioning everything she believes in. Falling for a wealthy playboy like Dane is against the rules, but if she's just faking it what's the harm?

Capturing Her Beauty

KAYLA REID HAS ALWAYS been into fashion and everything to do with it. Growing up wasn't easy for her. A bigger girl trying to squeeze into the fashion world is like trying to suck an entire gelatin mold through a straw; possible, but difficult.

She found herself an open door as a designer and jumped right in. Her designs always made the models smile. The colors, the fabrics, the styles. Never once did she dream of being on the other side of the lens. She got to watch her clothing strut around on others and that was good enough.

But who says you can't have a little fun when you're off the clock?

Sometimes trying on the latest fashions is just as good as making them. Kayla's hours in front of the mirror were a guilty pleasure.

A chance meeting with one of the company photographers may turn into more than just an impromptu photo shoot.

Hot n' Handsome, Rich & Single... how far are you willing to go?
MEET ALEX REID, CEO of Reid Enterprise. Billionaire extraordinaire, chiseled to perfection, panty-melter and currently single.

Learn about Alex Reid before he began Managing the Bosses. Alex Reid sits down for an interview with R&S.

His life style is like his handsome looks: hard, fast, breath-taking and out to play ball. He's risky, charming and determined.

How close to the edge is Alex willing to go? Will he stop at nothing to get what he wants?

Alex Reid is book 1 in the R&S Rich and Single Series. Fall in love with these hot and steamy men; all single, successful, and searching for love.

Book One is FREE!
SOMETIMES THE HEART needs a different kind of saving... find out if Charity Thompson will find a way of saving forever in this hospital setting Best-Selling Romance by Lexy Timms

MY SWEETHEART 191

Charity Thompson wants to save the world, one hospital at a time. Instead of finishing med school to become a doctor, she chooses a different path and raises money for hospitals – new wings, equipment, whatever they need. Except there is one hospital she would be happy to never set foot in again—her fathers. So of course, he hires her to create a gala for his sixty-fifth birthday. Charity can't say no. Now she is working in the one place she doesn't want to be. Except she's attracted to Dr. Elijah Bennet, the handsome playboy chief.

Will she ever prove to her father that's she's more than a med school dropout? Or will her attraction to Elijah keep her from repairing the one thing she desperately wants to fix?

HEART OF THE BATTLE Series

In a world plagued with darkness, she would be his salvation.

No one gave Erik a choice as to whether he would fight or not. Duty to the crown belonged to him, his father's legacy remaining beyond the grave.

Taken by the beauty of the countryside surrounding her, Linzi would do anything to protect her father's land. Britain is under attack and Scotland is next. At a time she should be focused on suitors, the men of her country have gone to war and she's left to stand alone.

Love will become available, but will passion at the touch of the enemy unravel her strong hold first?

THE RECRUITING TRIP

Aspiring college athlete Aileen Nessa is finding the recruiting process beyond daunting. Being ranked #10 in the world for the 100m hurdles at the age of eighteen is not a fluke, even though she believes that one race, where everything clicked magically together, might be. American universities don't seem to think so. Letters are pouring in from all over the country.

As she faces the challenge of differentiating between a college's genuine commitment to her or just empty promises from talent-seeking coaches, Aileen heads to the University of Gatica, a Division One school, on a recruiting trip. Her best friend dares her to go just to see the cute guys on the school's brochure.

The university's athletic program boasts one of the top hurdlers in the country. Tyler Jensen is the school's NCAA champion in the hurdles and Jim Thorpe recipient for top defensive back in football. His incredible blue-green eyes, confident smile and rock hard six pack abs mess with Aileen's concentration.

His offer to take her under his wing, should she choose to come to Gatica, is a temping proposition that has her wondering if she might be with an angel or making a deal with the devil himself.

THE ONE YOU CAN'T FORGET

Emily Rose Dougherty is a good Catholic girl from mythical Walkerville, CT. She had somehow managed to get herself into a heap trouble with the law, all because an ex-boyfriend has decided to make things difficult.

Luke "Spade" Wade owns a Motorcycle repair shop and is the Road Captain for Hades' Spawn MC. He's shocked when he reads in the paper that his old high school flame has been arrested. She's always been the one he couldn't forget.

Will destiny let them find each other again? Or what happened in the past, best left for the history books?

** This is book 1 of the Hades' Spawn MC Series. All your questions may not be answered in the first book.

FORTUNE RIDERS INC
BILLIONAIRE BIKER
LEXY TIMMS
Download For
FREE
Lexy
Timms

Fire HOUSE ROMANCE
CAUGHT in
FLAMES
BESTSELLING AUTHOR
LEXY TIMMS
LIMITED
TIME
Lexy
Timms
FREE
DOWNLOAD

MY SWEETHEART

Lexy
Timms
BOSS
Managing the Bosses: Book 1
Lexy
Timms
Grab your
copy today!

FOREVER
FOREVER
FOREVER
BOOK 3
BOOK 2
BOOK 1
Saving
FOREVER
Lexy
Timms
Limited
Time for
99cents

MY SWEETHEART

Did you love *My Sweetheart*? Then you should read *Highlander's Bride* by Lexy Timms!

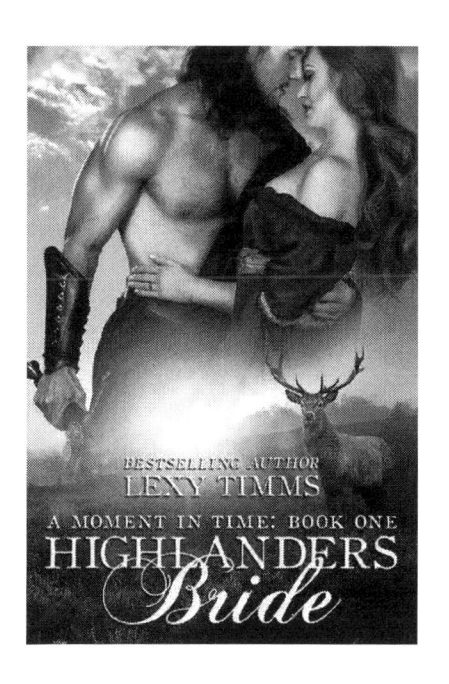

NEWLY UPDATED AND MORE STORY ADDED TO HIGHLANDER'S BRIDE!

One moment in time was all it took...

She shouldn't be here... She can't even recall how she got here.

Except for the dream. Mya Boyle remembers the dream. She knows it's somehow connected to her past, her present and the future.

Mya woke one morning in a field, a stag grazing close by as if it didn't even notice her. She lay bare, like a babe from the womb, except for a wool blanket wrapped around her tightly.

A grown woman with no memory, no family, no money, nothing. Kayden McGregor found her while hunting. He was after the stag and nearly shot her with his arrow instead. Unable to leave her to the wolves of his clan, he took her to his home.

He resents her. She can't bare to look at him. Or stop herself from staring when he doesn't notice. Trapped, and yet somehow destined to be together.

Remember enough of the past... You may be able to control your future.

Moment in Time Series:#1 - Highlander's Bride#2 - Victorian Bride#3 - Modern Bride

#4 - A Royal Bride

#5 - Forever the Bride

Read more at www.lexytimms.com.

Also by Lexy Timms

A Burning Love Series
Spark of Passion
Flame of Desire
Blaze of Ecstasy

A Chance at Forever Series
Forever Perfect
Forever Desired
Forever Together

A "Kind of" Billionaire
Taking a Risk
Safety in Numbers
Pretend You're Mine

BBW Romance Series
Capturing Her Beauty
Pursuing Her Dreams

Tracing Her Curves

Beating the Biker Series
Making Her His
Making the Break
Making of Them

Billionaire Banker Series
Banking on Him
Price of Passion
Investing in Love
Knowing Your Worth
Treasured Forever
Banking on Christmas

Billionaire Holiday Romance Series
Driving Home for Christmas
The Valentine Getaway
Cruising Love

Billionaire in Disguise Series
Facade
Illusion
Charade

Billionaire Secrets Series
The Secret
Freedom
Courage
Trust
Impulse
Billionaire Secrets Box Set Books #1-3

Branded Series
Money or Nothing
What People Say
Give and Take

Building Billions
Building Billions - Part 1
Building Billions - Part 2
Building Billions - Part 3

Change of Heart Series
The Heart Needs
The Heart Wants
The Heart Knows

Conquering Warrior Series

Ruthless

Counting the Billions
Counting the Days
Counting On You
Counting the Kisses

Diamond in the Rough Anthology
Billionaire Rock
Billionaire Rock - part 2

Dominating PA Series
Her Personal Assistant - Part 1
Her Personal Assistant Box Set

Fake Billionaire Series
Faking It
Temporary CEO
Caught in the Act
Never Tell A Lie
Fake Christmas
Fake Billionaire Box Set #1-3

Firehouse Romance Series

Caught in Flames
Burning With Desire
Craving the Heat
Firehouse Romance Complete Collection

For His Pleasure
Elizabeth
Georgia
Madison

Fortune Riders MC Series
Billionaire Biker
Billionaire Ransom
Billionaire Misery

Fragile Series
Fragile Touch
Fragile Kiss
Fragile Love

Hades' Spawn Motorcycle Club
One You Can't Forget
One That Got Away
One That Came Back
One You Never Leave
One Christmas Night

Hades' Spawn MC Complete Series

Hard Rocked Series
Rhyme
Harmony
Lyrics

Heart of Stone Series
The Protector
The Guardian
The Warrior

Heart of the Battle Series
Celtic Viking
Celtic Rune
Celtic Mann
Heart of the Battle Series Box Set

Heistdom Series
Master Thief
Goldmine
Diamond Heist
Smile For Me

Highlander Wolf Series
Pack Run
Pack Land
Pack Rules

Just About Series
About Love
About Truth
About Forever

Justice Series
Seeking Justice
Finding Justice
Chasing Justice
Pursuing Justice
Justice - Complete Series

Kissed by Billions
Kissed by Passion
Kissed by Desire
Kissed by Love

Love You Series
Love Life

Need Love
My Love

Managing the Billionaire
Never Enough
Worth the Cost
Secret Admirers
Chasing Affection
Pressing Romance
Timeless Memories

Managing the Bosses Series
The Boss
The Boss Too
Who's the Boss Now
Love the Boss
I Do the Boss
Wife to the Boss
Employed by the Boss
Brother to the Boss
Senior Advisor to the Boss
Forever the Boss
Christmas With the Boss
Billionaire in Control
Billionaire Makes Millions
Billionaire at Work
Precious Little Thing
Priceless Love
Gift for the Boss - Novella 3.5
Managing the Bosses Box Set #1-3

Model Mayhem Series
Shameless
Modesty
Imperfection

Moment in Time
Highlander's Bride
Victorian Bride
Modern Day Bride
A Royal Bride
Forever the Bride

My Best Friend's Sister
Hometown Calling
A Perfect Moment
Thrown in Together

Neverending Dream Series
Neverending Dream - Part 1
Neverending Dream - Part 2
Neverending Dream - Part 3
Neverending Dream - Part 4
Neverending Dream - Part 5

Outside the Octagon
Submit
Fight
Knockout

Protecting Diana Series
Her Bodyguard
Her Defender
Her Champion
Her Protector
Her Forever

Protecting Layla Series
His Mission
His Objective
His Devotion

Racing Hearts Series
Rush
Pace
Fast

Reverse Harem Series
Primals

Archaic
Unitary

RIP Series
Track the Ripper
Hunt the Ripper
Pursue the Ripper

R&S Rich and Single Series
Alex Reid
Parker

Saving Forever
Saving Forever - Part 1
Saving Forever - Part 2
Saving Forever - Part 3
Saving Forever - Part 4
Saving Forever - Part 5
Saving Forever - Part 6
Saving Forever Part 7
Saving Forever - Part 8
Saving Forever Boxset Books #1-3

Shifting Desires Series
Jungle Heat
Jungle Fever

Jungle Blaze

Southern Romance Series
Little Love Affair
Siege of the Heart
Freedom Forever
Soldier's Fortune

Spanked Series
Passion
Playmate
Pleasure

Spelling Love Series
The Author
The Book Boyfriend
The Words of Love

Taboo Wedding Series
He Loves Me Not
With This Ring
Happily Ever After

Tattooist Series

Confession of a Tattooist
Surrender of a Tattooist
Heart of a Tattooist
Hopes & Dreams of a Tattooist

Tennessee Romance
Whisky Lullaby
Whisky Melody
Whisky Harmony

The Bad Boy Alpha Club
Battle Lines - Part 1
Battle Lines

The Brush Of Love Series
Every Night
Every Day
Every Time
Every Way
Every Touch

The Debt
The Debt: Part 1 - Damn Horse
The Debt: Complete Collection

The Fire Inside Series
Dare Me
Defy Me
Burn Me

The Golden Mail
Hot Off the Press
Extra! Extra!
Read All About It
Stop the Press
Breaking News
This Just In

The Lucky Billionaire Series
Lucky Break
Streak of Luck
Lucky in Love

The Sound of Breaking Hearts Series
Disruption
Destroy
Devoted

The University of Gatica Series

The Recruiting Trip
Faster
Higher
Stronger
Dominate
No Rush
University of Gatica - The Complete Series

T.N.T. Series
Troubled Nate Thomas - Part 1
Troubled Nate Thomas - Part 2
Troubled Nate Thomas - Part 3

Undercover Series
Perfect For Me
Perfect For You
Perfect For Us

Unknown Identity Series
Unknown
Unpublished
Unexposed
Unsure
Unwritten
Unknown Identity Box Set: Books #1-3

Unlucky Series
Unlucky in Love
UnWanted
UnLoved Forever

War Torn Letters Series
My Sweetheart

Wet & Wild Series
Stormy Love
Savage Love
Secure Love

Worth It Series
Worth Billions
Worth Every Cent
Worth More Than Money

You & Me - A Bad Boy Romance
Just Me
Touch Me
Kiss Me

Standalone
Wash
Loving Charity
Summer Lovin'
Love & College
Billionaire Heart
First Love
Frisky and Fun Romance Box Collection
Beating Hades' Bikers

Watch for more at www.lexytimms.com.

About the Author

"Love should be something that lasts forever, not is lost forever." Visit USA TODAY BESTSELLING AUTHOR, LEXY TIMMS https://www.facebook.com/SavingForever *Please feel free to connect with me and share your comments. I love connecting with my readers.* Sign up for news and updates and freebies - I like spoiling my readers! http://eepurl.com/9i0vD website: www.lexytimms.com Dealing in Antique Jewelry and hanging out with her awesome hubby and three kids, Lexy Timms loves writing in her free time. MANAGING THE BOSSES is a bestselling 10-part series dipping into the lives of Alex Reid and Jamie Connors. Can a secretary really fall for her billionaire boss?

Read more at www.lexytimms.com.

Printed in Great Britain
by Amazon